The Snowball Effect

The Snowball Effect

Marlene Mesot

Print layout and e–book conversion by
DLD Books Editing and Self–Publishing Services
www.dldbooks.com

Unless otherwise noted, all scripture references are from the New American Standard Bible, Giant Print Edition, Thomas Nelson Publishers, The Lockman Foundation, LaHabra CA, ©1977.

ISBN: 978–1–7347393–7–4

4 Elements of Mystery Series

1. The Purging Fire
2. The Snowball Effect
3. Whirlwind of Fear
4. Terra Terror

More Mysteries

The Cat Stalker's Sonnets

Poetry

Edgy Poetry
The Author's Edge

www.marlsmenagerie.com

Romans 12:2

And be not conformed to this world, but be transformed by the renewing of your mind, that you may prove what the will of God is, that which is good and acceptable and perfect.

Contents

Contents

1
Memorable Meetings

"Ouch!"

"Oops, I'm terribly sorry. I wasn't looking where I was going." Melissa Marcus apologized quickly to the young woman she had just bumped into.

Recovering from her surprise the darker-complexioned woman stated, "Neither was I."

"Did I hurt you?" Missy asked. Her face felt hot.

"No, not at all." The other woman was smiling now and held out a white-gloved hand in Missy's general direction. "My name is Clara Méndez. I am waiting for my friend, Tom, who went to find our luggage."

Missy shook hands briefly and then introduced herself. "Yes, my husband Alex is doing the same thing. I'm Missy San—uh, Marcus. We were just married yesterday." Missy's heart leaped at the flash of white teeth and exclamation of joy from her new acquaintance. She continued to explain, "Anyway, Alex told me to wait over there, but I was just looking around, and I didn't know you were behind me. This airport is so big. It's my first flight. Again, I apologize, Clara. I should have been paying attention to where I was walking."

"No matter. I was just startled. I do not see at all."

"What?"

Clara explained, "I have been blind since birth."

"Oh, really? I couldn't tell. You see, I'm legally blind and I wear hearing aids," Missy told her.

"Melissa!"Alex's voice was sharper than usual.

"Alex, I'm over here." Missy turned her attention toward seeking her tall, blond husband among the crowd. She knew it was more concern than anger that had edged his voice. Alex was not over protective or overbearing, but he was realistic about her safety.

"Missy, I told you to wait for me over there."

"Yes, I know, darling. I was just trying to see, and, well I accidentally bumped into Clara, here. Clara is totally blind. Clara, this is my husband, Alex Marcus."

"Hello, Clara." The soft familiar warmth had returned to her spouse's voice. "Missy is blind in one eye, and she hears only what she wants to, most of the time."

Missy opened her mouth to protest but was interrupted by another male voice calling loudly.

"Clarissa! Where are you?"

"Here, Tom. I am still here." Clara called back. "That is my friend Tom Hawkins. We flew here together. We are going skiing."

Missy named the ski lodge where she and her new husband were going and asked if they were going to the same place. "Did you say your name is Clarissa Méndez?"

The dark haired woman nodded. "Si, Clara is for short."

"Alex." Missy's grip tightened noticeably on his arm.

Alex had been watching the fair–haired man pushing his way through the crowd toward them. "Probably coincidence, honey," he said without looking at his brown-haired wife.

The other man had reached them by now. Alex interpreted his stern expression as disapproval. When he spoke, however, his voice was even.

"Clarissa, you know you shouldn't talk to strangers."

"It's my fault," Missy offered, "I ran into her accidentally."

"Then you should look where you're going." Tom snapped.

Alex explained. "My wife doesn't see very well, either."

"Tom, do not be so critical." Clara countered. "I can take care of myself. Besides, these two are on their honeymoon, and they are going to the same place we are. So why not take the same taxi?"

"Sure, that sounds great." Missy agreed quickly. "I'd like to get to know you better while we're here. Where are you from, Clara?"

"Missy," Alex chided, "don't be so nosy. We're going to be there for two weeks. There's plenty of time. Let's get going."

"Take my arm, Clara."

"I know, Tom."

While they were riding to their destination Alex described the snow-covered beauty of the countryside for his wife and Clara, who was listening with interest. When Tom began to speak to her, she shushed him for interrupting Alex's details.

"Thank you, Alex," Clara said when he stopped talking. "You have a way with words. Why do you not explain things that way, Tom?"

"Snow is snow, Clara. No matter if it's here or back home in New York. You still have to shovel it, don't we, Alex?"

"Yeah, you've got that right." Alex agreed.

"Well, I like snow," Missy asserted. "It's fun."

"Not when you have to drive in it, lady," the cabbie said.

When they reached the resort, Doug Johnson, the innkeeper, greeted them at the door. He explained that orientation would take place promptly following breakfast the next morning. This day of arrival was a chance to meet the other guests and staff on an informal basis before the program commenced.

"Alex, I'm so excited!" Missy exclaimed while they were unpacking in their room. She continued to quickly fold and stuff her clothes into the bureau drawers. She didn't see her husband's soft smile.

Alex arranged his belongings in his methodical manner.

When Missy dropped her dress and coat hanger on the carpet, he came to pick it up for her. "Take your time, honey. We have plenty of time to do this. We're not going to a fire, you know."

As soon as the words were out, Alex fervently wished he could take them back.

"Not funny," Missy said and then frowned remembering. "Seems hard to believe that it's been two and a half years since that dreadful college semester."

Alex sighed and then said, "Honey, I'm sorry. It's just an expression."

He began to kiss her forehead, her face, gently, softly. He was determined to lighten her mood and not spoil the moment. He began to massage her shoulders. "Relax," he murmured as he pressed more fervent kisses to her neck. Then his hands embraced her tightly.

Finally she responded eagerly to Alex's embrace, and rested her cheek against the warm thickness of his knitted sweater. Missy wished she hadn't been reminded of the arsonist,

Arthur Wills, who had tried to kill her that semester, out of an unfounded delusion of prejudice. What coincidence could have brought him to the Iandale College Campus, the same deranged man who had tried to kill another blind girl by fire in high school for the same reason?

Missy raised her head to look up at her new husband. "Alex, we've got to find out if Clara Méndez is the same girl that Art tried to kill in high school. We know her name and that she's from New York. We just have to ask her—"

"Missy," Alex interrupted, "slow down. Don't let your imagination run away with you. I never asked for a description of the girl. We just had her name and the place it happened. Besides, we have more important things to think about." He began to nibble gently at her neck again.

A shiver ran down her spine as his breath tickled her skin. "That tickles." Delight sang in her voice. "Alex, shouldn't we go back down stairs?"

"Mm." He raised his head to kiss her lips. "In a while."

When they had organized themselves in their room, Clara and her roommate Marie LeBlanc sat on their beds to talk.

"So, you are legally blind, too, like Missy Marcus?" Clara asked. "Thank you for showing me around the room."

"Yes," Marie answered. "I'm blind in one eye and deaf in one ear. If you're on my right side, I probably won't respond to you. I can see just about enough to get around. I've been blind and deaf since I was born. What about you, Clara?"

Clara nodded and then spoke. "Yes, I was born blind. I see nothing, but my hearing is good. Now tell me what you look like, Marie. Your voice sounds young."

"Oh, boy. Well, I'm seventeen, and I'm blonde, green eyes,

and I'm white. My only ancestors come from France and Canada, but I am all American and don't speak a word of French. Mom and Dad are in the room across the hall if we need them, by the way."

Clara chuckled. "As American as apple pie, eh? My friend Tom Hawkins says that all the time. He is from New England. My family lives in Troy, New York. We are Hispanic, and, yes, I speak Spanish. I attended public high school there and then went on to graduate college in my home state. I have just finished doing some graduate work in dream research. I am still single and I felt it was time for a vacation, so I decided to come here to learn to ski. Now, it is your turn."

Marie giggled. "I still have next year to graduate high school, and I'm still single, too. Are you and Tom going steady?"

"Not if I can help it. No. We worked together at the University for Dream Research and we have gone out a few times. He insisted on coming out with me for this trip. Marie, do you like to listen to music? I mean, at night when you go to bed?'"

"Yeah, sure.'"

"I brought some special tapes with me, and if you like them, you can use them too. It is music with Bible verses added in, but only your subconscious mind can hear them. They help me to relax and sleep."

"Wow, I never heard of that before," Marie admitted.

"It is called subliminal suggestion, and it can be used for positive results, regardless of the spy movies images."

"Boy, I'd sure like to learn more about dream research and this sub, sub whatever you said stuff."

"Well, let us keep it between us, okay? I do not want everyone to know about it. What is our room number again? I forgot."

"Eight," Marie told her. "It's in large, black, raised numbers as well as braille on the door."

"That is good. I am glad we did not get number thirteen. I would hate that."

"Don't worry. My dad says hotels don't use number thirteen because it's unlucky. Are you superstitious, Clara?"

"I do not believe in taking chances where the stars are concerned. I believe in astrology, and I also believe in interpreting dreams. We can talk more later. I think it is getting near supper time." The cover of her braille watch clicked shut after her fingers had checked the time.

Alex and Missy were slightly embarrassed when applause met them at the bottom of the staircase. They were still holding hands.

"We thought you two deserved it since you're our only newlyweds this session." Sam Rosario, the speaker, walked toward them with hand extended toward Alex.

Alex took the darker hand and shook it warmly. He stared across into twinkling brown eyes set in a darker complexion. Alex guessed the man to be a few years his senior. Alex smiled amiably and introduced himself and his bride.

"I'm Sam Rosario, one of your guides." He then proceeded to introduce the other members of the staff and the rest of the small group.

Following breakfast the next morning, the people were divided into two groups, sighted guides and non-sighted trainees. The instructors' staff guides took each trainee individually on a mobility tour of the resort while Doug Johnson briefed the sighted partners, who had come voluntarily with the trainees, in most cases, on instructional procedure.

"Most of you know by now that I'm Doug Johnson, the owner and senior staff member. I'll be briefing you on technique and safety factors for teaching our friends fun and safe skiing." He craned his neck as he surveyed the faces gathered around him.

"If memory and my math serve me correctly, we are missing someone. Can anyone help me with a name?"

Looking around at the others, Alex recalled that Clara's friend was not present. "I think Tom Hawkins isn't here yet," Alex answered. "I remember him because he and Clara Méndez came with my wife and me in the same cab. We met at the airport."

Doug glanced at his watch. "Well, then, I'll start with an introduction and brief history of the program, and hopefully he'll arrive soon. I want to be sure that there's enough time for questions before the other group finishes their preliminary tour."

Doug had already begun his explanation of procedure when Tom finally joined them. Briefly Doug repeated the information and then went on.

"Trust is a key factor," he explained. "A person who is blind can learn to ski successfully with a sighted partner who verbally warns of obstacles in the path and gives proper cues for the skier to follow, such as, turn right 45 degrees, or all clear straight ahead for about 250 feet. You substitute for the eyes with verbal instruction. Now, first of all, we need to judge your proficiency at the sport, so you can keep up with your partner."

"Uh oh," Alex muttered.

"By a show of hands, please, how many of you have never skied before?" Doug queried.

Alex and a couple of the other people raised their hands.

Doug nodded. "Well, let's get dressed and head for the

slope."

Even before they had finished the tour of the premises, Clara decided that she was intrigued by Sam. His strong, assertive tone assured her that he felt comfortable with authority. From the direction of his voice, she sensed that he spent much of the time looking at her. The thought made her uncomfortable, but she dismissed it as part of his job.

"Now, Clara, it's time to test your memory." They had stopped walking. "We're at the foot of the stairs." He gently twisted his arm out of her grasp and then guided her hand to the railing. "I want you to lead me up to your room so that you can get your ski clothes to go outside for your first lesson."

"Really? We can start now? I have been looking forward to this for a long time. I am ready to go." She began to climb the steps quickly. When she stopped suddenly half way up the stairs, the man behind her bumped into her, as she half turned toward him.

"Oh, I'm sorry. I wasn't looking...expecting...Why did you stop, Clara?" Sam stammered.

Clara reached out to steady herself and rested her hands against his broad chest. His hands were at her elbows steadying her. Was that his heart or her own that she felt racing like a downhill skier in a meet? All of her senses seemed to be standing at attention, acutely aware of his closeness.

"I am sorry," she heard her voice say while her thoughts were trying to convince herself that she hadn't done it on purpose. "I just wanted to be sure you were coming behind me."

"You can count on it." The inflection in his voice indicated that he was smiling.

She pulled her hands back but he did not release her immediately.

Sam's voice was lower, softer when he spoke. "Clara, you

are very beautiful." Then he released her arms.

Shaking her head she turned abruptly to continue walking. "You do not know me, Sam."

At the top of the landing, Clara turned right and counted her paces to herself. This time she put out a hand to indicate she was stopping. "I have been practicing with Maria so I can do it by myself. Here is my room, number eight."

After she had unlocked and opened the door, she heard Sam gasp. "What is the matter?"

"It's been ransacked."

2
The Battle Begins

The remainder of the party continued on schedule with the exception of Marie, her parents, Clara, and Sam.

After the drawers had been replaced and their contents returned, Clara announced, "I cannot find my cassette tapes. They were in the bottom drawer of my bed stand."

"We'll have your door lock changed," Sam told them. "It was forced. I'll need a list of everything that's missing to show Doug."

Marie nodded. "Clara, are you sure you can't find any of them?"

"No, not one," she answered her roommate. "I had six relaxation tapes. I like to listen to them before I go to sleep at night."

"Marie, are you missing anything?"

"No, Dad. Even my diary is still here." She sat down on her bed. "That would be the first thing I'd take if I were going to steal something."

"Maria!" Her mother exclaimed.

"It's okay, Mrs. LeBlanc. Clara, what's so special about those tapes? " Sam asked.

"They are relaxation music with Bible verses added to them that only your subconscious mind can hear. You can buy them anywhere." She explained.

"And you're missing nothing else?" Sam asked.

"Yes. I already said that," Clara answered.

"Marie, maybe you can help Clara search again later, just to be absolutely sure," her father suggested.

"Sure, I will, Dad. I'm sorry, Clara."

"I know. Me, too." Clara sighed. "Well, Sam, I guess we go skiing now?"

"We should get started. By the way, let's keep this incident to ourselves. I have to tell Doug, but no one else. Understand?" Sam queried.

"Don't worry. I can keep a secret." Marie stated proudly. "I haven't told anyone about what Cla—"

"Marie!" Clara spoke sharply.

"Oops. I was just going to say that I didn't say anything." She made a face.

Following the morning lesson Clara cajoled Sam into giving her a few extra minutes of free time on the beginner slope while the rest of the group went inside to settle down to lunch. Sam stayed with her to watch. Clara was determined to put her fears, disappointments, and problems aside to enjoy the freedom of movement this new venture would bring her.

"I am ready Sam. May I go now?"

Adding a final reassuring boost of confidence, Sam asserted, "That's right, Clara. You have plenty of wide open space all around you. There's just a small pitch downhill and then you'll level off. Go!"

Clara dug her poles into the snow ahead of her and slid forward. With back and knees bent slightly, she began to glide downward. The wind whipped the tassel of her stocking hat and sent her hair out behind her in a black stream.

Sam smiled, watching her successful descent. He understood the confidence and new feeling of freedom this would give her. He didn't realize how captivating his thoughts of her had become until she repeated her call.

"Sam, which way do I go?"

Hearing the crunch of footsteps off to her left, she turned toward the sound.

"Magnificent!" Sam called as he approached her. When he reached her he took her arm to guide her off the trail in order for her to walk back up the hill sideways. She was still wearing skis.

"One more time, please Sam? I love it! And I did it myself!"

"You were a natural, just great, Clara. I love watching you."

"Oh?" Why was she trying to make more of his statement, she asked herself silently.

"Grace and beauty are a powerful combination."

Clara's expression sobered. "I tell you, beauty is deceptive, and grace, well, that is up to Jesus Christ."

"Yes, I know this too," Sam replied. "I have experienced His love."

Her sharp intake of breath betrayed her surprise. Then she asked, "How did you become a teacher for the blind?"

"Let's just say that I like to help people. Actually, I have two jobs. I'm a paramedic, also. I work for the county fire and rescue squad, second shift. You see, I work here and then at my other job each on alternate weekends. So it keeps me busy."

"I guess so."

They had reached the top of the hill by now.

"And you, Clara? What made you decide to come here?" Sam asked in turn.

"I needed a vacation," she responded truthfully.

"From what?"

"That could be a long story. I have been doing some work with dream research, and I felt that it was time for a change. Tom insisted on coming out here with me. He is a lab technician from the university where the research was being conducted."

"Are you dating?" Sam asked.

It was a casual question, but Clara reacted with resentment. "Certainly not. He knows too much...I mean, he knows me very well, and I have no desire to be that close with him. I keep telling him that he is not my keeper. Why do you ask, anyway?"

"Just wondered. After your last run, we'd better go get some lunch."

Clara nodded and then poised herself to concentrate on her descent.

When they entered the dining room, Clara asked Sam to guide her to where she heard Missy and Alex talking together.

"Hi, Clara, Sam," Alex greeted them. "Have a seat and join us."

"Thank you, Sam. I will see you later for another lesson, okay?"

Taking the hint, Sam excused himself and left their table while Clara sat in the chair that Alex held for her.

"Clara, is everything all right?" Missy asked her.

"Yes. I just felt that I would enjoy spending some time with you, Missy."

"If you ladies will excuse me I'll be back in a few minutes."

"Oh, no, Alex. Do not leave. I am sorry," Clara apologized.

Missy nodded to her husband as he left to go to the bathroom. "It's okay, Clara. He's just going to take his medication in private. It's his habit. Is something bothering you?"

"Men. They ask too many questions sometimes. I have already told Marie more than I should have about myself." She sighed then continued. "Why does everybody think that I am dating Tom? Just because we came together, that does not mean anything. I really do not like Tom that much, anyway. He is too bossy sometimes, you know?"

"Yeah, I understand. Here comes your lunch and our desserts," Missy told her. "Don't worry. You can trust Alex and me to keep a confidence. He's a practicing psychologist. He even has his master's degree in psychology, and I have a bachelor's in teaching. I am a special education teacher. We met when we were at college together in Iandale, New Hampshire. You wouldn't believe how we got together. Where are you from, Clara?"

"I have a Bachelor of Arts in languages. After graduation I went to the University of New York to work with dream research. I am from Troy, New York, actually."

The spoon that Missy had just dropped clattered to the floor. "Sorry. I'm clumsy." Missy bent down to pick it up and then wipe it with her napkin.

"It comes naturally to us, do you not think so?" Clara asked.

"Yes. That's what I keep telling Alex. Here he comes now. Alex, guess what? Clara is from Troy, New York. Did you know that?"

"Then we're practically neighbors. I hope you told her that we're New Englanders," Alex said casually.

"Oh, yes," his wife replied.

"I think Tom is from New England." Clara speared a piece of meat. "I seem to remember that he said he was from somewhere in Vermont."

"You must really enjoy skiing, to come in this late for lunch," Missy ventured. "Or is it the instructor?"

"You know, I have never skied before, and I love it already. Sam said I have very good balance. It is so new to have such free movement."

"I can relate to that, Clara. Alex and I have a special bicycle built for two that we enjoy riding. Alex always takes the front to drive it, of course."

"That is wonderful. How do you like skiing, Alex?" Clara asked him.

"The battle begins," he responded. "I have a balance issue because of my epilepsy. I don't have the grace of you two lovely ladies."

Clara's expression sobered. "I am not lovely, Alex, but thank you, anyway."

"Oh, Clara—" Alex's touch indicated to Missy not to push the matter. "Well, this is a perfect honeymoon for me," Missy continued. "I think I'll enjoy snow skiing just as much as water skiing."

"You water ski, too?"

Missy nodded. Then, correcting herself, she answered verbally. "My grandparents own a camp on a small lake, and I've been water skiing since I was about twelve, I guess. Alex will drive the motor boat, but I haven't gotten him to try it yet."

"I may still be on the beginner slope when we leave, but I'll keep at it," Alex promised.

"That is right, and keep trying. Do not give up," Clara encouraged him. "Alex, did you know that Sam is a paramedic? Maybe you should tell him about your condition just in case, you know?"

"In case I have a seizure. Yeah, the staff knows. Luckily I haven't had one in almost a year, now, since the doctors finally found a dosage that works for me. I take my medication three times a day with meals so that I don't forget."

Missy leaned closer to her husband in order to whisper in his ear. "I love you." Then she turned back to finish her tea.

"I would like to go upstairs for a few minutes," Clara said.

"No dessert?" Missy asked.

Clara shook her head and stood. "I need to check something."

"We'll go with you," Alex offered. "We could go back to our room for a few minutes before the next lesson begins."

As they approached the landing Alex saw Tom Hawkins coming down the hallway toward them. He didn't miss the surprised expression on Tom's face when he saw them together.

"Well, if it isn't Clara and the, uh, honeymoon couple." Tom put a hand into the oversized pocket of his sweater as he spoke. "I'm sorry. I can't seem to recall your names at the moment."

Missy felt a blush beginning to creep up her cheeks.

"Alex and Missy Marcus," Alex supplied. "Coming from Vermont, you must be an old pro at this sport."

"Ha! Not to brag, but I grew up in ski country. I hear you two are practically neighbors, from New Hampshire?"

Alex nodded.

"Never been there. Clara, can I talk to you?"

Tom followed closely behind her as Clara went to unlock her room door and go inside it.

Once inside their room, Missy asked, "Now, just what did you have in mind, Mr. Marcus? We don't have much time."

"Mm, I know. Come sit here with me." He extended his long arms to pull her down onto his lap in the armchair where he was sitting. "I just wanted to steal a few minutes alone with you."

Pleasure surged as she responded to his kiss.

Then he told her, "You are my confidence, darling."

"But the joy of the Lord is your strength, love," she reminded.

"I know." His lips sought hers again. "I thank God that He gave you to me."

She hugged him tightly and prayed in an unsteady whisper, "Thank you, Jesus, for our commitment in your sight. May it never be spoiled or broken. Amen."

They held each other in silence for a time.

"What do you want, Tom?" Clara asked impatiently.

"Hey, what's the rush? Where's your little roommate, what's her name?"

"Marie? She is probably with her parents. Tom, I want to be alone for awhile."

She could smell his aftershave and feel his body heat when he stepped close to her. Clara felt warm, strong fingertips under her chin.

"No problem, my little rose. I just wanted to remind you about taking your sleep medication. You agreed to start taking it once we arrived here. Remember?"

"Yes, I remember. I had hoped that I could do without it. Now, let go of me, please. You know that I do not like to be touched."

Tom dropped his hand. Then he said, "You're not being smart about this if you want to get rid of those nightmares.

You've come this far. It would be a shame to lose ground now. I'll see you later tonight, and maybe we can discuss it again huh?"

"Maybe. Now please go." She went into the bathroom.

Several moments of silence were followed by a clattering, rattling noise, then silence again. She couldn't tell if she had heard the click of the door.

Clara opened the bathroom door and called Tom's name. There was no answer. She decided to go and get someone sighted to look around, just to be sure that nothing else had been taken or disturbed. She went out into the hall and walked slowly, feeling for the room number eleven. She knocked.

"Come in," Missy called.

"I hope I am not intruding." Clara said as she closed the door behind her. "Alex, I would like you to look in my room for me. I thought I heard a noise while I was in the bathroom after Tom left, and I just want to be sure that everything is okay."

"Be glad to, Clara." Alex tried to make his tone sound reassuring. "Are you ready, honey?"

Missy nodded.

Upon searching Clara's room, Alex found everything to be in order except that one of the nightstand drawers had been left open. When he tried to close it, something stopped him. He removed the drawer and set it down on the bed. "Your cassette tapes must have fallen behind it," Alex explained. "That's why you couldn't close this drawer all the way."

"What? My tapes? Let me have them." Clara, with a bewildered expression, held out her hands to receive her lost items.

Alex placed six plastic boxes into her possession. Clara ran her fingers over the familiar braille name labels that she had stuck to the sides of each box identifying them as her personal property. "I don't believe it!" she exclaimed.

"What's the matter, Clara?" Missy asked.

Clara shook her head. "You do not understand." She sank down to sit on her bed. She dropped the small boxes onto the pink bedspread. "You said that I can trust you two to keep a secret."

"Of course you can," Alex answered. He went to sit in a nearby chair while Missy sat on the bed beside their new friend.

"How can we help you?" Missy asked.

Clara sighed and then began to briefly explain. "When Sam and I returned here this morning after the tour, we found that my door lock had been forced, and when we entered, the room was a mess. My roommate, Marie LeBlanc, and her parents helped us straighten up. The only things missing seemed to be my relaxation tapes. And now you find them here, after all. I am confused."

"Clara, did you—I mean, did Sam see anyone in the hall this morning when you came back here?" Alex asked her.

Clara shook her head. "I reported these tapes missing, and now they are here. I feel foolish."

"No, Clara." Missy patted her hand gently. "They were in a very obscure place. Were they sermon tapes?"

"No. They are scripture songs with Bible verses in them that only your subconscious mind can hear. They are relaxation tapes," Clara explained again.

"Oh, yeah, I've heard of that, but I never bought one. Could I borrow one?"

"Missy," Alex admonished her boldness.

"No problem, Alex. Which one would you like to use, Missy?"

"This one sounds good: *Trust God*. I'll give it back to you tomorrow morning, I promise, Clara. Thank you." Missy put the tape box in her purse.

"Clara, would you like me to talk to Sam?" Alex offered.

"I was not supposed to talk to anyone, Alex. I do not know what to say to that."

"Tell Sam that you talked to us, or to Alex, and see if Sam approaches him," Missy suggested. "Believe me, Alex is a super detective. Why, he and his friend Pete Early pr—"

"Missy, I don't think Clara needs any more problems right now," Alex stopped her. "Our past isn't important, anyway."

"Thank you, both of you, for your help. I am glad to know that my tapes are safe. Well, I think we should be going downstairs now." Clara stood.

That evening following supper, Alex and Missy joined the informal social gathering in the large meeting room. Sam was absent because of his second job, but Clara was also not attending.

"Tom," Alex asked, "have you seen Clara this evening?"

Tom shook his head. "No, but I plan to look in on her before I turn in tonight. By the way, Alex, I hope you have a better day on the slopes tomorrow," he grinned, scoffing.

"Hey, you're not the only one, Alex. Don't let him bug ya."

Missy recognized the loud tones of Burt Franklin, one of the other trainees who was blind. When standing, Burt stood tall and slender. His russet hair and red-faced features gave him an out-of-doors rugged appearance.

"The battle begins," Alex teased. "Hey, Burt."

"Just don't carry that attitude into the bedroom, eh?" Burt jibed.

Alex watched his wife's expression change as she pressed her lips into a straight line. She hadn't made up her mind if she really disliked Burt or not, yet.

Ray Powell, a middle–aged staff instructor, suggested a sing–along, to which everyone present agreed. Missy urged her husband to go upstairs and get his guitar, as Ray did also. Another trainee who was also totally blind, Brenda Lacey, volunteered to accompany on the piano in the meeting room. Once she heard the singing, Clara came downstairs to join in the group festivities.

True to his word, Tom escorted Clara upstairs when she excused herself because she was ready to retire for the evening.

"Mind if I come in for a few minutes?" Tom asked from the doorway.

"All right." Clara agreed.

He strode over to a desk chair deliberately making it squeak so that she would know where he was sitting. "Clara, you know I wouldn't bring up unpleasant memories if I didn't care about helping you. I really think you should take the medicine for your own good. Haven't you suffered enough from your trauma?"

"I know, but I wish I did not have to take anything. I just wish I could go back to living a normal life. I had hoped that my new relaxation tapes would be enough to get me through the rough nights."

"Yes, I see." Tom chose his words carefully. "You told me when you bought the tape set, but you want to be sure, don't you?"

She nodded and then looked up. "I did? Funny, I do not remember telling you about these tapes. In fact, I just bought them the day before we were to leave to come here...I think. Wasn't it?"

"Trust me, Clara. You're getting confused already. Now, go and get the bottle and take your pill. It's for your own good."

She obeyed him.

"That's right. Things will work out. You'll see. Trust me, Clara." Again he tilted her chin upward. "I wouldn't lie. I wouldn't give you a snow job." After a short pause he said, "You'll play the Positive Thinking tape tonight. Pleasant dreams."

Tom placed a light kiss on her forehead and then released her chin. He turned to leave her room.

3
A Different Nightmare

Clara sat on the edge of the bed and ran her hand down to the bottom drawer of the night stand. Opening it, she removed the tapes.

There are only five here, she counted to herself. Where is the other one?

Panic threatened her for a moment. Then she remembered that she had loaned it to Missy. She ran her fingers over the labels to check the titles. Yes, *Trusting God* was missing.

At that moment, the door opened and Marie announced her presence. "I was afraid I would wake you. I'm glad you're still up, Clara."

"Uh, I thought I would wait until you came back before I went to sleep." It sounded like a good excuse. Clara didn't want to say that she had forgotten about her roommate since Tom's visit. Realizing that Marie was still speaking to her, Clara looked up from her lap. "What did you say? I am sorry, I was not paying attention."

"I said, are you all right? You look...puzzled."

"No, just preoccupied. Oh, by the way, look what I found."

Clara held up the tape boxes.

"Oh, wow! That's great. Where were they? We looked all over. I just can't imagine that they were here all the time."

"Me, too. They were behind the bottom drawer here in the night stand." She pulled out the bottom drawer to show Marie. "Strange, though."

"I'll say." Marie agreed. "Does Doug know that you found them?"

Clara nodded. "Do you mind if I play one while I go to sleep? It helps me relax. I'll keep the volume low."

"Oh, I don't mind at all. I usually fall asleep with the radio on anyway," Marie said. "Which one are you going to play?"

"It's music," Clara explained. "You won't hear the underlying message, but your subconscious mind may. This one is called *Positive Thinking*."

"That's good stuff. We all need more of that." Marie took her night clothes into the bathroom to shower and change.

Clara set up her tape recorder and inserted the tape so that it would be already playing when she finished her shower in turn.

While they slept, the masked message that had been superimposed onto the tape kept repeating intermittently the phrase "snow job." Only Clara's preconditioned mind was susceptible to its implied submission of obedience to the user of the trigger phrase.

"Missy, come sit down. I want to talk to you." Alex led her to the arm chair, and he took the desk chair and straddled it to face her. "If Clara is the same girl that was injured in the high school fire caused by Arthur Wills, let her approach us if she wants to talk. You should know that you can cause more harm than good if you push too fast. No one here needs to know about our dealings with him in college, either. We have to gain Clara's trust."

"Yes, doctor. Alex, I know you're right. I just feel that she's desperately seeking help. She seems to be awfully confused. One minute, she's strong, assertive, and independent and the next, she can't remember what she did a few hours ago. Do you think those tapes were ever missing?"

Alex didn't answer immediately. "I don't know. She swears to it, but it doesn't appear so. Then, why would only her tapes be taken? One thing is certain, though. Sam says that her door lock was definitely forced open."

"Why would somebody want to search her room?" Missy pondered.

Alex folded his arms across his chest. "Don't know."

"Well, I know there is more to Clara Méndez than meets the eye."

"Oh, is that supposed to be a pun?" Alex asked playfully.

"Very funny," his wife retorted. "Just because I had one play published, that doesn't make me a writer."

"And just because I solved one mystery, that doesn't make me a super, what do you call it, sleuth, either."

Missy leaned forward as she spoke in soft, sweet tones. "Ah, but you are, and always will be, my hero." Her lips approached his with tenderness.

Alex unfolded his arms to embrace his wife, drawing her closely against the chair back that came between them. A broad smile began to creep across his lips. She couldn't see the sparkle of happiness that shone in his blue eyes. "You make me feel so special, Missy, and I'm not."

"You are special, darling, and not just to me. You are fearfully and wonderfully made in His image," Missy quoted from the Bible.

Silently, with his eyes never leaving her, Alex rose to set the chair aside. Then, taking her hands, he gently pulled her to her feet and led her toward the bed.

Before getting into bed, Missy quickly slid the cassette tape into her radio recorder and turned it on. While they cherished each other, and then while they slept, the added message suggested to their subconscious minds ,"trust Tom."

That evening Clara's nightmare returned. Again she heard the fierce crackling sound and felt the intense heat of the fire. She knew she was back in the high school gymnasium, trapped by flames and panic. She stumbled and felt she was falling. Then she was lying flat on her back, unable to move. The hard surface under her lent a coldness in contrast to the heat that she felt on her face.

The dream had never taken this turn before. This was a different nightmare. An antiseptic smell tingled her nostrils. Clara gasped when a harsh raspy voice broke the silence.

"Repeat it, Clara!" it commanded.

"I will obey all commands," she heard her own voice saying.

"If you do not, you know the consequences."

After the raspy voice came the smell of smoke and the heat closer to her face. Clara couldn't move her arms or legs. Her body seemed to be paralyzed. Fear tried to snatch away her reasoning. She remembered all too well the periods of intense pain and the slow skin grafting process that she had undergone following the actual fire during her last year of high school. Some of the scars were permanent, weren't they?

The voice cut into her thoughts again as easily as a knife slices through a banana. "You will remember nothing of this incident. It will be completely erased from your mind Do you understand?"

"Yes," she heard herself answer automatically.

Again dizziness claimed her. The words became a haunting echo. "You will not remember." She tried to cry out to stop the words but there was no relief. "You will not remember."

"Remember what?" her mind asked. Remember... Remember...

The solid pressure of a warm touch finally roused Clara to wakefulness. She sat up, unable to think, and waited.

"Clara, it's okay now. You had a bad dream. It's Marie, your roommate."

"Marie?"

"Yes. You're at the ski lodge. Remember?"

Clara grabbed the hand that still held her arm. "Don't say that word. I will not remember!"

"What?"

"Oh, nothing. I'm confused. I had a terrible dream. I'm not thinking clearly. Excuse me."

Clara heard the click as Marie stopped the tape and the music abruptly ceased. "No, I must play it." Clara felt for the machine on the night stand and started it again. "Oh, I mean, I would like to listen to it while we get ready, if you don't mind. That dream really scared me. I need something to take my mind off it so I can forget about it."

"Sure, that's okay," Marie said. "But it isn't time to get up yet. I'm going back to bed now."

Clara felt the mattress rise slightly when the younger girl rose.

"Don't worry, Clara. I'll wake you if you yell again," Marie assured her.

4
Blind Fear

Alex pointed toward the table where Clara and Tom were eating breakfast when they entered the dining room the following morning. "Let's join Clara and Tom. Oh, and here comes Sam, too." Alex lifted a hand in greeting.

"So you're really gonna try it again Alex?" Tom teased.

Alex nodded and grinned faintly.

"He may surprise you today, Tom," Sam encouraged. Turning his head he asked in a softer voice, "How are you today, Clara?"

"Ready to go. I want to ski as well as Tom by the end of this vacation. You watch me."

"You can count on that," Sam promised.

"Well, when do I get to pair up with her?" Tom asked.

"Probably not until next week at the earliest. Doug is a tough taskmaster. You sighted guides will practically have to be able to ski in your sleep before he has confidence to give you a blind partner. Safety takes priority," Sam explained.

"Absolutely," Tom was quick to agree.

"Sam, do you think we could go out for another private

lesson during lunch period, please?" Clara begged.

"What's this?" Tom asked.

Clara turned toward him. "Never mind, Tom. This is between Sam and me." She turned back. "Please, Sam?"

"It would be my pleasure, lovely lady."

Sam's soft voice whispered tenderness and seemed oddly comforting to her troubled spirit.

Tom's chair snarled its protest when he pushed it back to allow him to stand. "If you people will excuse me, I'm going to check my equipment before exercises. Clara, you be careful." He picked up his tray and left the table.

"Tom really cares about you, doesn't he?" Missy asked Clara. This morning, Missy had an affectionate attitude toward Tom's directness.

"We've been through a lot together. He knows me too well."

Sam reached over to touch her hand for a moment. "I'd like to get to know you better, Clara. Your enthusiasm brings a new dimension to the sport for me."

Missy looked at her husband and smiled.

Alex leaned back in his chair and folded his arms across his chest. He shook his head slightly and then turned to look at Clara. He had watched her rubbing her eyes. He wondered if he should venture to ask her what was causing her to lose sleep.

"Alex," Missy asked, "are you going to take your medicine?"

"In a minute." He uncrossed his arms to pick up his juice glass and finish it. "I'll be right back. Does anyone want anything?"

"Another raspberry tart and tea?" his wife asked. She saw him smile as he reached for her cup and left the table.

"Clara," Sam asked, "would you like me to ask Doug if I can be your instructor? He should be assigning a permanent pairing of staff instructors to trainees today for your one-to-one training."

His voice sounded hopeful to Missy.

"Yes, I believe I would like that," Clara agreed.

"Great." The inflection in Sam's voice reflected his eagerness as well. He also rose to leave the table. "Excuse me. I'll go and arrange it with Doug now."

When the two young women were left alone, Missy exclaimed, "My goodness, Clara, it looks as if you have two suitors."

Clara shook her head in quick denial. "Oh, no, no. You misunderstand, Missy."

"I don't think so. I didn't think any guy could be interested in me, either, and look what happened."

Clara giggled. It was a nice, pleasant sound. "You really think so?" she asked.

"Believe it," Missy encouraged her.

"Is Alex still here?" Clara asked.

"He went to take his medication. He'll be right back."

Clara sighed. "I wish I could sleep better. I feel so dragged out."

"Is something bothering you?" Missy prompted.

"I keep having nightmares. They're very strange dreams."

"Do you want to tell me about them?" Missy asked.

"I don't know. Tom says that I shouldn't talk about them."

"Why not?"

"Well—" Clara stopped speaking when she heard a plate being set on the table. "Alex is back?"

"Yes, Clara," he responded amiably. "I brought you some fresh coffee and another pastry."

"Thank you, but I'm not really hungry. I'll just drink the coffee."

"Okay, then. I'll take your tart, if you don't mind."

Clara nodded. "I was telling Missy that nightmares keep me awake at night. I wish I could sleep better."

"You do look tired," Alex said.

Clara moaned a little. "I'm getting a headache, too."

"Alex, let's pray," Missy suggested earnestly.

He nodded and took Missy's outstretched hand. "Clara, give us your hands. Reach out under the table, and we'll pray with you."

Clara took their hands while Alex prayed softly for God's intervention and direction on her life.

When he had finished, she thanked him meekly.

"It's our privilege," Alex assured her. "God cares about all of His people, no matter what circumstances they are in. I learned that one the hard way."

"I think I'll start over to the meeting room now." Clara stood and picked up her breakfast tray. "Thank you again, Alex and Missy." She started to move slowly, sliding her cane along the floor for guidance.

When she had walked away, Alex turned to his bride. "How about a little encouragement before I have to leave you for the morning?"

Missy smiled and put her arms around Alex's neck. "You don't need any encouragement." She raised her face to his.

"Oh yeah?" He dipped his head to meet her kiss. "Lots." He kissed his new wife again.

Alex pulled back as wood slapped against his ankle and his identification bracelet jingled. "Ow!" he exclaimed in surprise.

"Oops. Sorry, Alex. What in the world is that sound?" Burt stopped just short of collision.

"It's my medical alert identification ankle bracelet," Alex told him.

"Sorry. I didn't know you were there."

"That's all right," Missy answered.

"You're supposed to watch where I'm going," Burt asserted loudly. Then he continued to tap along his route with his cane.

"Guess we'd better get movin', honey," Missy said as she stood.

"Right. See you later, love," her husband answered.

They went to their separate instruction areas.

The morning was spent becoming familiar with the ski equipment, how to check it and care for it. Again, Sam and Clara came in late for lunch. Afternoon practice went as smooth as ice.

At the dance that evening, the festivities began with a waltz. The newlyweds were invited to lead with the first dance. As they walked slowly onto the open floor, Missy protested.

"Alex, everyone will be looking at us."

He squeezed her hand and then faced her to encircle her back with his other hand. "Don't worry, darling, it will be fine. Just concentrate on me."

He smiled as the corners of her mouth turned upward slightly, warming his heart. His arm gently coaxed her hand inward, against his chest, where he entrapped it. They moved slowly and gracefully, preoccupied with each other, not really concentrating on where they were going, lost in the moment.

The applause captured their attention, halting their memories, calling them back to the present, and ceased their descent into oneness for the time being.

Now Doug was inviting the guests and the rest of the staff to join in.

"Hey, Brenda, let's show 'em how it's done." Burt had stood and was waiting for a reply.

"Uh, Burt," Doug suggested, "why don't you try it with

Marie first?" Doug kept his eyes on Marie's parents, who were giving each other questioning glances.

Marie took her cue and walked over to the older man. "Don't worry, Burt. I won't step on your toes."

He laughed and reached out to take her elbow, allowing her to lead him onto the dance floor. Her parents and several other couples joined them and the Marcuses as the music resumed.

"Clara, it would be my honor to dance with you."

"Sam? But I thought you had another job in the evening."

"I do get days, or nights, off once in a while, you know." He took her hand and drew her up from the chair into an infinite warmth that she could not explain to herself.

Tom got up and walked over to a bewildered–looking Brenda. "Hi, Brenda. If you'd like to dance with me, I promise I won't bump you into anybody. I'm Tom."

"Yes. Thank you for asking me, Tom." Her smile was shy.

Sam and Clara glided smoothly around the floor like two skiers traveling a familiar path. Clara felt as if a weight had been lifted from her shoulders, allowing her spirit to climb. She was breathless when the dance finished. "Sam, that was wonderful."

The next dance was a faster pace.

"Missy, how about you and me this time?" Burt asked. "Come on. What do you say?"

Missy looked at Alex and began to shake her head. "I don't know."

"How about it? Ol' Burt's a pretty good stepper, even if I do say so myself," Burt persisted. "Alex won't mind this once. Right Alex?"

"I don't usually dance with strange men." Missy blurted out.

"No problem. I'm not strange," Burt countered. "How 'bout it?"

"I—I meant that I don't usually dance with guys that I don't know very well," Missy amended.

"Go ahead, honey, just once." Alex urged her to go ahead and get it over with, and then maybe Burt would leave her alone after that.

Missy made a face in her husband's direction and walked over to where Burt was waiting. "Okay, Burt, just this one dance."

"Great. Gotta keep up my image, you know."

"Alex, I hear you need a partner?"

He turned to see Brenda shift her feet uncertainly as if she was uncomfortable. Desiring to build her confidence, he tried to make his voice as earnest as possible. "My pleasure Brenda."

He reached for her hand to lead her onto the floor. Alex could see the same self-conscious stiffness in Brenda's movements as he had seen in Missy's except when he held his wife. "Relax, Brenda. You're doing fine. How do you like your skiing lessons?"

"Oh, it's fun. I ski better than I dance."

"You'll get better with practice. I dance better than I ski," he told her truthfully.

"Really? I didn't think that sighted people would have any trouble."

"Skiing is a matter of balance, and mine is sometimes off."

When the music finished, Alex escorted Brenda back to her seat and thanked her for the dance. Then he set out to find Tom.

"You got a minute, Tom? I've been meaning to have a word with you."

"Guess so." Tom walked with him out into the hallway.

"I don't mean to be too forward," Alex began, "but I'm a practicing psychologist. I was wondering how much you know about Clara Méndez's past."

"Why?"

Alex hesitated in order to choose his words carefully. "I have my reasons. I'll explain after you answer the question. My interest is to help her face her problems."

"Hmm." Tom pulled on his chin with the tips of his long, slender fingers. It was an unconscious gesture. "So she didn't fool you with her independent air? Well, I assume that you won't break a confidence?"

"Of course I wouldn't. My wife and I are completely trustworthy. You have my word on that."

"What does your wife have to do with this?"

"She's involved with Clara's past, more so than I am."

Tom released his chin to shove his right hand into the side pocket of his pants. "Well, I don't want to betray Clara's trust, you understand, but she came to the university to be the research subject, not to conduct the research. She has undergone hypnotherapy as a dream research subject to alleviate nightmares that resulted from a past tragedy."

Alex nodded. "Go on."

"She was severely burned in a fire when she was in high school, and she still has reoccurring nightmares about it. I'm a technician from the dream research lab keeping her under observation while she's on vacation. Of course I'm in constant contact with her physician back at the university." Tom didn't supply the physician's name.

"Then you do know about Arthur Wills?"

Tom's eyebrows rose in a gesture of surprise. "How do you know that name?"

It was Alex's turn to explain. "He was my college roommate when I was an undergraduate. He tried to kill my then ex-fiancée, Missy, by arson. That's how we found out about his attempt on Clara. You can imagine our surprise when we literally bumped into her at the airport."

Tom's expression clearly indicated surprise. "I had no idea."

"Now you know where I'm coming from. If we can be of help to Clara in any way, we will. She seems to be pretty open to talking with Missy. You know how women are."

"Mm." Tom's hand went to his chin again and pulled. Following several moments of silence, Tom finally spoke. "You said ex–fiancée. You mean you've been engaged to her twice?"

"Yeah, you could say that. It's another long story that I don't need to go into right now. It isn't relevant to the situation at hand, anyway. I guess I'd better go find my wife before she thinks that I've deserted her. Be glad to help, Tom."

"I will definitely keep you in mind, Alex. Count on it." Tom raised his hand in salutation as Alex walked away.

When Alex reentered the large meeting room, he found his wife sitting with Clara and Sam, talking together.

"Well, Alex, we were thinking of sending the rescue squad out to find you," Sam teased.

"Alex, where did you go?" Missy sounded upset.

"I saw you were busy, so I took the opportunity to have a chat with Tom."

"What on earth for?" Clara asked. Concern edged her voice.

"Oh, just one professional to another." Alex sat on a chair near his wife's. "I was curious about his work."

"He just hooks up machines and takes readings," Clara said.

"That can be interesting to another technician," Sam observed.

"Well you could have at least told me that you were going out for a while," Missy protested.

"Sorry, honey. I didn't think you would miss me." Alex leaned closer to his wife so that she could see his face. He was smiling innocently.

"Yeah, well, don't try to make up to me."

"Clara, may I have another dance?" Sam asked. He was already on his feet in front of her as soon as the music began to play again.

Clara stood, smiling happily, and took his lead.

"May I have this dance, fair lady?"

Missy sighed at her husband's use of his affectionate term for her and stood to put her hand in his. On the dance floor, she kept her outstretched hand rigid and tried to maintain a casual embrace with the other arm.

Alex leaned close and dipped his head near to her ear. Her hearing aid squealed at his nearness, but he still spoke softly but clearly into it. "You were right about Clara."

"What?"

His affection toward her ear sent shivers down her spine.

"Tom knows all about Art Wills, and Tom is trying to help Clara deal with her past. I was just talking to him alone. That was where I went earlier, to find Tom."

"Oh, I knew it!" Missy released his hand to hug him with both arms.

He drew his head back to face her. "Does this mean that we're friends again?"

"Better than that, darling." He didn't miss the twinkle in her eyes. "We're lovers."

"Is it always that easy to make up?" Sam tried to sound innocent when the four of them sat down again.

Alex shrugged silently and made a face, causing Sam to chuckle softly.

"Where's Tom?" Clara asked.

"I think he went to make a phone call," Alex answered her.

Sam turned his attention back to Clara. "Are you having a

good time, Clara? I know I'm enjoying your company very much."

"Oh, yes, thank you. But it still isn't as good as skiing."

Alex grinned and then said, "Well, I don't feel that way."

"Your right of preference is fine," Sam agreed, "but you are here for skiing lessons, and in that, you have no other choice."

"Mm. Well, on that note I think we'll turn in," Alex replied.

Sam and Clara seemed hardly to notice when Alex and Missy got up to leave the room.

"When will we start on steeper hills?" Clara was asking Sam.

"Each trainee works individually with his or her instructor. We go steeper when I say you're ready to go." Sam's heart warmed at her delighted smile. "Clara, I have never had such an eager student."

"I love the feeling of freedom when I glide downhill. I've never known such pleasure. It's like casting all of your cares to the wind and concentrating on being carefree for that moment."

"Cast all your cares upon Him," Sam quoted softly.

"What?"

"Oh, it's a quote from Scripture."

She grunted. "I believe, but I don't read it."

"You can. There are Bibles in braille, on tape, and even computer disks."

Clara shrugged. "I just never looked into it. I have a phone number for my horoscope, though. I call it every day."

"Oh, no. You really believe in that silly superstition?"

"It is not silly superstition," she retorted. "It's the truth Besides, it works."

"God's Word is the truth," Sam said. "It can set you free."

"I am free, Sam. I choose to believe in astrology, and I do."

Sam sighed his disapproval.

Clara stood and stretched her white cane out in front of her. "Good night, Sam. I can find my own way upstairs. Thank you." With that said, she tapped on her way.

Once on the landing upstairs, she turned right to follow the short railing along, counting her paces. Then she turned to cross the hallway to feel for her door number. Yes, she had stopped across from Number Eight.

Finding it locked, she began to fish in her purse for her key. She opened the door to be greeted by a hot, stuffy room. After closing the door quietly, she stood for a moment leaning against it.

She barely noticed the music playing softly. Surely I did not leave my recorder on? she asked herself silently. No, I remember. It's playing the *Spiritual Gifts* tape. Why, I know I was not even playing that one!

Bewilderment flipped her stomach into fear when she heard the crackling sound. Panic seized her.

Clara turned, struggled with the door knob, and finally got it open. Slamming it behind her, she started across the hallway to grip the short railing.

"Sam! Sam! Come quick!" Her voice was strained.

The sound of running steps matched the pounding of her heart, and Sam was soon beside her trembling body, asking what was wrong.

"Fire! In my room!" she stammered.

Sam took the key from her clenched hand and went to open the door.

5
Skiing Free

As if the words had not penetrated the walls of her mind, Clara made Sam repeat what he had just said.

"There is no fire, Clara," Sam reiterated patiently. "There's nothing unusual in your room at all. I've searched it thoroughly."

She felt grateful for his strength, for the warm hands that were supporting her arms, as her body seemed to suddenly become very pliable. The scent of his aftershave seemed to add to her dizziness. Sam was speaking to others, but her thoughts were not on them. Finally, her voice, a hoarse sob, pleaded, "But...Sam, I heard it. I heard the crackle of the flames, and I felt the heat. I know...and the music."

Sam half-carried her into the room. "Come with me, Clara. I'll show you. There's no fire and no music. You don't have a tape in your player, and your radio isn't turned on."

Sam managed to pry one of her hands free from his arm, and he walked with her slowly around the room, guiding her reluctant hand to touch items and surfaces in order to convince Clara of reality. When they had finished examining the last area, the bathroom, he led her back to the center of the room. "There, you see? Nothing is wrong."

"But...I heard it," she insisted. "I wouldn't have made up such a thing. It's impossible." Unconsciously she began to beat on his chest with her fists. "I couldn't. I'm not going crazy!"

To ward off hysteria, Sam slapped her face once, a stinging blow.

Clara caught her breath and stood still, dropping her hands to her sides and staring at nothing.

Sam's fingers touched his lips as he stared at the doll-like figure before him.

Lord, forgive me, he prayed silently. I thought I was doing the right thing. Finally he spoke. "Clara, are you okay?"

"Yes." The response was a monotone.

"Clara? Clara, I'm sorry. You were getting hysterical. Clara?" Tentatively he reached out to touch the cheek that he had struck.

Her eyes blinked and her mouth twitched. His name became a soft sigh. Then his lips were pressing against hers, inviting her into calmness. When they drew apart, his fingers were still caressing her cheek.

"Thank you, Sam." There was genuine beauty in her smile.

"Is it safe to leave you now? I think Marie's waiting with her parents across the hall. I can go and get her."

As he pulled his hand away, she caught his fingers and touched them to her lips to brush them gently. "You make me so confused. You know that? Sometimes I feel I want to run to you, and then other times, I run away from you, Sam."

Chuckling softly, he leaned forward to place a gentle kiss on her forehead. Then he pulled back and turned to leave. "Sweet dreams." He tossed the words over his shoulder before opening and then closing the door behind him.

When Marie knocked and entered, Clara was pushing a

tape into her player. She got into bed after clamping the lid of the player closed and pulled the bed covers up snugly around her neck. She hadn't even bothered to check the label to know which tape had been sitting out on her night stand or why.

"Good night, Marie." Clara said it as an afterthought.

"Good night, Clara," Marie called from the bathroom.

But Clara's dreams were not sweet as the subliminal message in her *Spiritual Gifts* recording repeated relentlessly, "Don't quench the fire." Her mind heard the crackling of flames, which reminded her subconscious of her past.

Following a restless night of fitful nightmares, Clara was anxious to get back to the slopes, where she could forget her fears and be skiing free. To her delight, she, along with Missy and Burt, was advanced to the next level, where they could try skiing on a steeper downhill run. Sam would still be her guide.

"Missy, you're doing great!" instructor Sandra Evans declared when her student had successfully completed a zig–zag course that had been sectioned off by guide ropes.

"Thanks," Missy acknowledged breathlessly. "I wish I knew how Alex is doing." She drew in a deep breath of air.

Sandy smiled and then replied, "You know what they say about patience. Maybe you could ask Doug about having a private session during free time with him."

"Really? I hadn't thought of that."

"It seems to work for Clara, huh?" Sandy answered.

It was Missy's turn to smile. "Why, Sandy, are you hinting at something?"

The instructor shrugged her shoulders with the swish of nylon from her parka. "What do you, think Missy?"

Missy sniffed and then answered. "Female student likes

male instructor, even if she doesn't know it herself yet." Then she added to herself, "Sounds like someone else I know." She remembered how she had been in self-denial about her feelings for Alex at first.

Sandy patted her student's shoulder in response. "Now, Missy, I'm going to ski down the hill. When I call you, I want you to come after me. Then I want you to turn and stop when I direct you. All right? Are you ready to go?"

Missy nodded and then watched as the other woman descended and moved gracefully downward. As she got farther and farther away, Sandy began to look like a black stick-shaped figure to Missy. Missy blinked her eyes, straining to keep her instructor in sight, but Sandy had moved too far away, out of Missy's range of vision.

Missy stood hesitantly waiting. Finally, she heard a short, high-pitched sound that she interpreted as Sandy's go-ahead signal. Missy descended, gliding easily over the white carpeting under her skis. She heard the command to turn right, which she did, and then to stop, which she easily executed.

"Missy, that was excellent! You'll be on your own in no time!" Sandy's enthusiasm excited the young bride.

"I can't wait to tell Alex."

Sandy nodded and then suggested that they start back up the slope, as it was nearing lunch time.

"Oh, already?" Missy complained. "Now I wish it was afternoon. This is great fun."

Later, when Missy entered the dining room, she recognized Sam's voice calling to her to join him. He and Clara were already seated.

"You look happy today, Missy," Sam observed.

"Oh, I love it! Sandy says I'm doing great. Sam, let me know when you see Alex. How are you doing, Clara?"

Clara sighed and then answered. "The skiing is great. I just wish that I could sleep better at night. I'm still having nightmares."

"That's too bad," Missy said. She thanked the waitress who brought her food and drink. Missy poured her tea water carefully and then began to dunk her tea bag thoughtfully. She pulled it up and then let it down into the water several times. Then she asked, "Clara, have you tried reading—uh—or listening to the Bible before you go to bed? It's available on tape as well as in braille, you know."

Clara shook her head. "No. I thought that my relaxation tapes would help, but they don't seem to be doing that."

"I can get you a set of Bible cassettes," Sam offered.

Clara shrugged and bit into her roll.

"I'll see what I can do," Sam promised. Then he added, "Clara, you have excellent balance and control on the slope, too."

Clara grunted. "Yes. It's just the rest of my life that's all mixed up."

"Trust in the Lord," Missy encouraged, "and He will direct your paths. You're not alone, Clara. Don't forget that."

"Yes, thank you, Missy. I feel better talking to you."

"Excuse me, ladies." Sam rose to leave the table.

As Alex entered the room, Sam approached and said something to him quietly. The two men walked out into the hallway and went up stairs.

"This is my room. Come on in and have a seat my friend," Sam invited.

"I'm glad you asked me up here, Sam. I've been wanting to talk to you alone. But you go first."

Sam sat down slowly on his bed, while Alex stretched out

on the desk chair.

"I don't know exactly what I'm asking," Sam began. "We really don't have much time. We'll be missed, not to mention missing lunch, but I thought I might impose on your professional opinion, if I may. I've always been a reader. I was the oldest in a large family, and I started working while I was still in school. I even helped take care of my grandmother when she lost her sight later in life. Anyway, I didn't spend much time chasing girls...and...well...what do you make of Clara?"

Alex chuckled. "You're not speaking to a man of the world here, either. My disability seemed to be in the way when I was attempting to date. When I finally did meet someone who truly understood me, I pushed her away with my blind self-pity. I couldn't admit to myself that someone could actually love me for who I really was. That's how Missy and I got engaged twice. She learned of my condition the hard way."

Sam had sat listening intently with his hands folded in his lap. His gaze was fixed on the younger man's fair features. "Go on, Alex," Sam encouraged.

"Missy found out that I have epilepsy when I had a convulsive seizure while we were bike riding. I had forgotten to take my medication, and, well, you know the rest. Only, instead of accepting her understanding, I got angry and frustrated at her. It took a near-fatal accident to make me realize how stupid my behavior had been. I thank God for her every day, Sam."

"Alex, that's remarkable." Sam's voice was quietly humble. After a pause, he asked, "How did you know that you loved Missy?"

Alex crossed his arms thoughtfully over his chest. "Well, there's the physical longing. To have and to hold, as they say."

Sam grinned.

Alex continued, "When I wasn't with her, I wanted to be.

Then, when I was with her, I felt complete. I had an overpowering urge to protect her, because there was real physical danger, as well. The most striking thing, I guess, is that she reminded me of my mother, who was deceased by the time I met Missy. My wife has a servant's heart, and she truly loves the Lord. But we have our differences also."

Sam nodded. "I can't figure out my feelings when I'm around Clara. She's beautiful. Her enthusiasm for skiing puts the sport in a whole new light. But I don't know how to take her. One minute, we get along great, and the next, she's fighting me. Last night, I hit her, and then I kissed her. I wasn't planning to. It just happened."

Alex laughed at Sam's bewildered expression, and then he jested, "Sounds like you've got all the symptoms, Sam."

Sam shook his head. "That's not what I wanted to ask you, exactly. I'm seriously worried about Clara. I've never seen anyone in such an emotional state. Last night, she insisted that there was a fire in her room, and she was getting hysterical over it. That's when I slapped her cheek, and the next thing I knew, I was kissing her. Anyway, this isn't the first time she's imagined something that isn't true. It just isn't normal. How can I help her, Alex?"

"She probably has a phobia, an unreasonable fear, of fire from her past, the accident when she was in high school, burned in a fire. Time, along with understanding and patient reassurance, should help. It takes some people longer to adjust to traumatic experiences than others. We all have different stress and tolerance levels."

Sam nodded. "Thanks. We'd better get back down stairs."

"Oh, there's something I wanted to ask you, Sam."

Sam stood and placed his hands on his hips. "Sure."

"I wonder how someone with poor sight or no sight has the

courage to attempt skiing. It's hard enough for me to do it. I'd like to try an experiment, if I could. Missy keeps saying that she can't wait to ski with me. Could you arrange perhaps for us to sneak some time together under your supervision, maybe during free time?"

"I'll try." Sam smiled remembering Clara's eager pleas. "Now, let's go get some lunch, if there's any left."

Alex smiled and nodded as they headed out to go back downstairs.

"Where have you been?" Missy queried as soon as her husband sat down beside her.

"Sam and I were having a man–to–man talk, darling."

"Uh oh. Clara, watch out," Missy warned.

"How's the skiing, Missy?" Sam asked her.

"Oh, wonderful." Missy beamed at the chance to elaborate. "I seem to be getting the feel of it. I wish I could show Alex."

Her husband grinned, but she did not notice it.

"Be careful, Missy," Clara said. "Your pride is showing."

Sam waved a hand above his plate. "Don't worry about it, Missy. You have reason to be proud, and so do you, Clara. You're very graceful on skis."

"Thanks."

"Alex, how do you like it?" Missy asked.

"Oh, I'm getting better. You'll see."

That evening, when Sam returned to the lodge after his shift at the fire station, he found Alex watching the news, with Missy asleep beside him, with her head on his shoulder. Sam stepped into the room and greeted Alex quietly.

"Are you sure we can go out this late at night?" Alex asked him.

Sam nodded. "I told Doug about it, and he said that we could. I'll meet you two out front, okay?"

Alex nodded.

Sam left to get ready.

When Alex pulled his arm free from behind Missy's neck, prickly pins ran along it. He nudged his wife and called to her several times.

Finally she stirred and sat up rubbing her eyes. "Going to bed now?" she asked sleepily.

"No," he replied.

"Huh?"

"Come on, we're going skiing." He stood and waited.

"What?" She looked up at him.

"Come on, sleepy head. I want to see how good you are."

She stood and took his arm, thinking he was just joking. But when he led her to get their ski jackets and gear, she knew he was serious. Sam met them at the front door.

"Sam?" she asked.

"Yes, I'm here to chaperone you two. You're off the regular trails, Missy, here out front. I want you to stay here near the front of the lodge, where there's enough light for me to watch you."

"Are you awake now?" Alex teased.

She nodded. Enthusiasm sparkled in her eyes.

"Missy," her husband said, "I want to understand how it is for a person who's blind to be able to experience skiing. I'm going to put on this blindfold, and I want you to direct me." He did so and then pulled down his goggles.

"What's the matter?" he asked when he heard her shaky intake of breath.

"Alex, you trust me that much?" She was almost crying.

"Don't worry, honey. Sam is on the porch, and he's a

paramedic. Remember?"

She nodded.

"Missy?"

"Yes, darling. I'm right here."

Alex shook his head. "No, no. Where is here? Be specific."

"Hmph." She thought, Now he's even acting like me. Collecting her concentration, she said aloud, "Okay, Alex, I'm going to turn you around so that you don't know which direction you're facing."

Missy guided his waist as he turned slowly by picking up his feet and walking his skis around. After a full turn and a little more, she told him to stand still. "All right. Now listen to my skis slide on the snow as I move away from you. When I call, I want you to ski toward me. Now I'm going to turn and go."

In the still night air, Alex could hear the hiss of wood slithering away and the crunch of her ski poles in the packed snow. Finally her voice beckoned him from off to his left.

"I hope it isn't too steep," he called back. "Here goes."

Alex slid one leg forward and then the other. He repeated the process and gradually began to move forward.

"Keep your legs closer together, Alex." Sam's voice came from the same direction that Melissa's had earlier.

She wasn't leading him into the building was she? "Missy?" Alex called.

From behind her, Sam urged Missy to keep talking to her husband. "Your voice is his guide line," Sam explained to her.

"That's right, Alex. Keep coming straight ahead."

"Where's the hill?" Alex called back.

"Right there."

For a few seconds, Alex glided, no longer needing his poles to push him along.

"Stop, Alex."

Alex thrust his ski poles into the snow and almost fell forward in his attempt to obey. He could feel the warmth of her closeness as Missy put her arms around him and gave him a swift kiss.

"Did I pass?" he asked.

"Yes, indeed," Sam told him.

Alex reached up to pull off his goggles and remove his blindfold. "I thought you were leading me into the building when I heard Sam give me instructions. I didn't hear him leave the porch."

"That's because you were paying attention to your instructor," Sam explained. "It shows good control and trust. Okay, Missy, now show us what you can do, and do it without the blindfold, please."

Missy smiled and went to the porch to put on her skis. She pointed to an easy slope off to their right and then started off.

Alex and Sam smiled as they watched her balanced display of confidence.

Once she had finished her run, the three of them prepared to turn in for the night.

Alex and Missy were about halfway up the stairs when Sam called them back.

"What is it, Sam?" Alex asked as they approached the front door.

"Look outside. Someone is coming in here," Sam said as he opened the door.

Alex turned his attention to the approaching footsteps from the staircase inside.

Tom was descending the stairs behind Alex's position on the staircase.

"What on earth is going on?" Tom asked. "I thought I heard voices down here."

All were silent while the shadowed figure stepped into the room from the porch through the opened door. As it approached into the lighted hallway, everyone could see clearly that it was Clara, dressed in night gown and robe, but she had come in through the snow barefoot.

6

A Clash of Wills

"Clara!" Missy exclaimed. "What on earth are you doing?"

Clara walked slowly, deliberately past the small group of guests without response, as if they were not there at all.

Alex touched Sam's arm and jerked his head slightly. This indicated to Sam that he was to notice Clara's facial features. "Hypnosis," Alex whispered close to Sam's ear.

"I'm afraid Clara is sleep walking again," Tom explained. Then he spoke in a matter-of-fact tone to the woman. "Aren't you Clara?"

"Yes, Tom." The two syllables were uttered in a low, even tone.

"Come with me, Clara. I'll see you to your room." Tom gently touched her elbow and began to slowly guide her toward the stairs.

Missy couldn't distinguish the words that her husband and Sam were whispering to each other as Tom and Clara ascended the steps. Deciding to follow her own curiosity, Missy touched her husband's arm and then turned to follow the pair upstairs to the second floor. As Missy was unlocking the door to her room, she overheard Tom speaking to Clara in front of the room next door, but across the hall.

He said, "Good night, Clara. Trust God."

Tom walked away to go to his own room, which was farther down the hallway.

Missy went into her room and closed the door, pondering Tom's statement. A short time later, when she heard her husband enter the room, Missy put down her book.

"Missy, are you still awake?"

She smiled and reminded him, "I already had my nap while you were watching TV. I didn't know Clara was a somnambulist."

"It looked more like a hypnotic state to me," Alex said. "The whites of her eyes were bloodshot, and she moved very slowly. Her voice was a monotone."

Missy cocked her head thoughtfully. "Hm. So you think Tom hypnotized her?"

Alex came to get into bed when he was ready. "No, I doubt it. Tom is only a technician, remember. Any hypnotizing would have been done by a doctor at the university. I think it was self-hypnosis."

"Really? I know she's into astrology, but that, too?"

"Why not? I certainly don't think that anyone else would have sent her outside barefoot in the winter." Alex settled down onto his pillow. "I'm tired, so good night, honey."

Missy turned off her reading light and lay down beside her husband. "Alex?"

"What is it, sweetheart?"

"Do you think Tom is a Christian?"

"How should I know?"

"I certainly wouldn't expect him—"

"Missy, get to the point."

"When I came up here earlier, I heard Tom tell her to trust God when he said good night. I just thought it was strange for him to say that."

"Well, it is good advice," Alex answered.

Some time had passed when Alex was startled awake by his wife's voice calling his name. He half rose under the bed covers. "What's wrong?"

"Nothing. I just realized something."

He dropped back onto the pillow with a sigh.

"Alex, the words 'trust God.' That's the title of the tape that I borrowed from Clara that day. Maybe it's more significant than just Biblical messages. He must have been suggesting that she listen to that tape."

"I'm too tired to think about it now. Good night, Missy."

She leaned over to give him a light kiss on his cheek, then she lay down to sleep.

When Alex and Missy entered the dining room the next morning, Alex could hear Burt's unmistakable laugh above the flurry of other conversations in the room. Alex pointed to a middle table where Sam and Clara were sitting.

"Well, here they are," Sam exclaimed as the two sat down with them. "You two are the last ones to come down. Breakfast is almost over. Oversleep?"

"Something like that," Alex said and grinned at Sam.

Missy ignored him. "Morning, Clara."

Clara made a sound of response and continued to chew her biscuit sandwich.

Alex looked at Sam. "I suppose she doesn't remember anything?"

Sam nodded before answering him. "Please tell Clara that

I'm not crazy."

"It's true, Clara. Alex and I also saw you. Even Tom was there."

Clara raised her head slightly and seemed to look at Missy. "Tom? Why?"

"I guess he heard us and came to see what the commotion was about," Alex supplied. "Sam, please pass me the butter."

Sam complied.

Clara shook her head in denial. "I don't remember ever doing such a thing as going out barefoot in the snow."

"Clara, have you ever been hypnotized?" Alex tried to ask the question casually, but his gaze was fixed on her face.

Clara nodded and then asked why he wanted to know.

"Just wondered," Alex replied carefully.

"It was some time ago. Not recently, anyway," Clara answered.

Missy replaced her tea cup on its saucer and tried to tactfully change the subject. "Well, I'm looking forward to another ski run. Aren't you, Clara?"

"Right now is fine with me." Clara stood. "I'm finished here." She began to move away from the table to exit the room.

"Eat up, slowpoke," Alex teased his wife. "I'll see you later." He got up to head out also.

"Missy," Sam said, "I really want to help Clara, but I'm confused."

Missy sighed and then answered simply, "Pray, Sam."

Once outside, Missy followed Sandy, her instructor, to another part of the ski area. "I think you're ready to advance to another part of the course on a steeper slope," Sandy told her student confidently. Then she explained. "It will take more skill to stop at a steeper angle with more speed, so stay focused and concentrate on what you're doing. You have plenty of room. Go ahead."

At first Missy, was a little overwhelmed at the opportunity she had been given. With practice, her confidence began to grow. After catching her breath, Missy thanked Sandy for the opportunity and expressed her pleasure on one of her later runs.

"You're doing fine, too. How about one more time, and then we'll break for lunch?"

"Oh, it's that late already?" Missy asked. "Has anyone else advanced like me? I can't wait to tell Alex about today."

Sandy answered, "Ray Powell is instructing Burt off to our left, but he and I can see each other from where we're standing."

Missy nodded and poised herself for the descent.

Sandy's expression changed from a smile to one of alarm when she heard the altercation between the other two who were practicing. She heard Ray yell to Burt to stop, and then Burt's response.

"No problem, teach." Burt kept going.

"Missy, stop! Missy!" Sandy's alarming call was of no use.

Missy had descended faster than Sandy had anticipated. Because of her hearing loss, Missy was unable to discern the words that were being hurled at her. Missy didn't see Burt, who was fast approaching on her blind side and of course Burt wasn't aware of her proximity crossing his path.

Abruptly, something slammed into Missy from her left. Both bodies lost balance and control to topple and then roll at the mercy of the slanting hill.

Missy's body stilled when she rolled against the trunk of a tree and hit her head on it. Another jolt from behind indicated to her that she had cushioned Burt's landing. Through the ringing in her head she heard Burt stammering.

Burt scrambled to stand sputtering. "I—I didn't know

anyone was in my way. Are you okay? Who are you, anyway?"

Stunned by the abrupt turn of events, Missy lay silently.

Sandy was beside her in seconds and reprimanding Burt, who was already stating his lack of injury with arrogant confidence.

By the time Ray arrived with Sam and Alex, Missy was sitting up, leaning against the tree. "I've lost a hearing aid," she complained.

"Here, honey, I've got it." Alex handed it to her as he stooped down beside his wife. "Are you hurt, darling?"

"I just hit my head. I think I'm okay."

After examining her, Sam suggested that she might have a slight concussion and that rest would be a good idea, but not sleep. Sam offered to bring a stretcher for her, but Missy protested, saying that she thought she could walk.

By the time they got back to the lodge, she was feeling dizzy and weak.

Ray had gathered up the lost equipment and come in behind them. Burt had arrived ahead of the others.

"Alex, what are you doing?"

He had scooped her up into his arms and was beginning to climb the stairs to their room. Once she had been settled into bed as comfortably as possible, he went to bring up their lunch trays.

"Sweetheart, you're spoiling me," she said.

Alex was propping and fluffing her pillows behind her before he set the tray in front of her. "Complaining?"

She shook her head, and a stab of pain shot through it. "Ow. No."

"I don't understand what possesses Burt to be so willful," Alex said.

Missy made a sound and continued to chew her food. They

continued to eat in silence for a few minutes until a knock at the door sounded.

Alex pushed back the desk chair and rose to answer it. He greeted the woman standing on the other side when he opened it. "Clara, come in."

"Thank you, Alex. I hope I am not disturbing Missy." She took several steps into the room.

"I'm glad to see you, Clara," Missy responded. "I just got a nasty bump on the head. I'll be okay once I get rid of this headache."

Following the sound of her friend's voice, Clara stepped closer to the bed. "I thought this might help you to relax." She held out the palm-sized, rectangular plastic box. "It's my *Spiritual Gifts* tape. You can borrow it."

Missy took the box. "Yeah, thank you, Clara. We enjoyed the one on *Trusting God*. Didn't we Alex?"

"Yes. Thank you for being so thoughtful, Clara. We'll probably get some of these tapes for ourselves when we get back home. In fact, I may even recommend them to clients."

"Clara, do they have any on marriage?" Missy asked.

Her friend smiled and nodded.

"Alex, I don't feel like eating any more right now. Would you take this tray away, please?"

"Sure, honey. Clara, if you don't mind carrying one, I'll walk downstairs with you. Missy needs to rest." He gave his wife a gentle kiss then left the room with Clara.

Missy opened the box, took out the cassette, and slid it into her radio recorder on her night stand. When it started to play, she adjusted the volume so that it was quietly comfortable but loud enough for her to distinguish the melody. Then she lay back and hugged her pillows while she silently thanked God for her husband's loving attentiveness and waited for sleep.

Following the afternoon lesson, when Alex returned to the room, he could hear his wife calling his name and crying out loud. As he walked toward the bed he realized that she was talking in her sleep.

"Alex...help...Can't...quench...the...fire!" She was lying on her back.

Alex tried to gently shake her to wakefulness. "Missy, wake up. Missy, it's all right. I'm here, darling. Missy, you're dreaming."

With a cry, she bolted upright and opened her eyes. Spontaneously, she clung to her husband's reassuring presence and began kissing him.

His arms around her tightened momentarily and he murmured her name as she nuzzled his neck. Her hands rubbing his back under his shirt felt exhilarating. Alex gave no heed to the music that was playing or its subliminal suggestion, "Don't quench the fire," as his bride stirred his emotions. The heat of their desires rose swiftly with the speed of a burning fire. And the two became one flesh, fulfilling their passions in the heat of the moment with fervent love.

Later, Missy turned her head upon his chest and reached over to stop the tape.

He gently wiped perspiration from her forehead with his palm. "You okay?"

She drew in a deep breath then answered, "My head feels like it's about to burst, but I feel wonderful, darling." She felt rather than heard his chuckle of satisfaction as his chest heaved slightly under her.

"That must have been some dream," he said.

She shifted her weight in his arms before replying. "It was a nightmare, and then when I saw you after dreaming that you were gone, it was just overwhelming...and, well, you know..."

He gently stroked her hair. "You were talking in your sleep again. What was the dream about?"

"For some reason, I was dreaming about the fire in my dorm room on campus at Iandale State. Then when I awoke and saw you, it was like waking up in the hospital afterward when we got reengaged. Remember?"

His lips told her wordlessly that he did. His hand continued to stroke her hair soothingly. "When I came in before, you were mumbling something about you couldn't quench the fire. Do you remember, darling?"

"Hm. That's odd. No, I don't really remember anything like that."

"Can you sit up, Missy?"

"I don't want to." Her eyes looked up toward his face. She could not see the twinkle in his eyes, but he was smiling. After he withdrew his embrace he turned on his side and she slipped to the sheet.

"Come on, now," he said, "we need to get ready for supper. I think you can manage a trip downstairs, huh?"

She sat up obediently. "I guess so. But I like having you wait on me."

He smiled. "Come on, I think you've been spoiled enough for one day. Let's go take a shower."

7
The Misfortune Teller

During the party that evening, Missy had been praying for God's sustaining grace to alleviate her throbbing headache. The warmth of Alex's touch made her blink, recalling her thoughts.

"Feel up to a slow dance? They're playing our song."

She smiled and listened to the instrumental opening to "My Special Angel."

"Only with you, sweetheart. I love this song." Missy stood to join him.

"I love my special angel." He led her out onto the floor.

"Marie?" Clara called.

"Right here, Clara."

"Would you guide me to the punch bowl?"

"Sure," Marie answered.

"May I serve you ladies?"

Clara recognized the voice of Doug Johnson's wife, Gloria, when they had reached the table.

"That's nice," Clara said. "I thought it was self-service."

"It gives our guests more independence this way. Ah, for Marie, fruit punch." Gloria scooped from the bowl to her left.

"Clara, would you like something stronger?"

"No, thank you. Fruit punch will be fine." She held out one hand to receive the glass.

Looking closely at Clara's palm, Gloria Johnson made a grunting sound.

"What is it?" Clara asked.

"Oh, I was just looking at your lifeline in your palm," the older woman replied. "Sorry."

"No, please tell me. You read palms? Thank you, Marie. I can find my own way back to my seat."

"Okay. See ya." Marie walked over to the food area.

After Marie had gone, the other woman spoke to Clara. "I see trouble in your future. Doug doesn't like me to use my abilities, but I won't refuse someone who's willing to know."

Clara nodded. "Yes, I'm a firm believer. What kind of trouble?"

"I can't say."

"May I meet with you in private?" Clara asked.

"Yes, we can arrange it. Someone else is coming. Hello, Tom. May I serve you?" Gloria smiled pleasantly. She was pleased that she had found an audience.

"Sure. I'll have some of that." He pointed to the other punch bowl. "Then I'd like to dance with Clara."

Gloria sipped her own drink quietly. From her other side, she heard Sam's voice.

"I was about to ask Clara the same thing."

Clara felt the heat of a blush rising in her cheeks. "My goodness. Ah, Sam, do you mind if I dance with Tom first?"

"Of course he doesn't," Tom answered for him. "Shall we?"

"You're such a good dancer, Tom," Clara observed as he guided her artfully around the floor.

"And you've learned your lessons well, Clara."

"Tom, school is over, so don't go around telling tales, please."

"Don't worry, my little rose, I have everything under control." After a short pause, he asked, "How are those nightmares?"

Her eyebrows rose, betraying her surprise. "How did you know?"

"That you still have them? I know all about you, Clara."

"You scare me when you talk like that, Tom."

Tom spun her around with the ease of spinning a toy top and then brought her back close to him. Her steps faltered slightly but he held her firmly. Finally he spoke again. "So, Clara, are you still taking your sleeping medication every night?"

"Yes, of course," she answered breathlessly.

"And the nightmares?"

"Yes, they're about the fire. I can't seem to stop them. I don't know why the tapes aren't helping me, but Missy and Alex enjoyed them."

Tom almost missed his step, but he caught himself. "What did you say?"

"I lent a couple of tapes to Missy, and she and Alex—"

"Which tapes?" Tom demanded.

"Why should you care?" Clara countered defiantly.

Tom sighed and led her to an empty corner of the room when the dance had finished. In a quieter tone, he said to her, "Now, Clara, don't give me a snow job." After a few seconds pause, he asked again which tapes she had lent out.

Obediently, she answered, "*Trust God,* and just today, *Spiritual Gifts.*"

"Clara, you will not lend any tapes to anyone for the remainder of this trip. Do you understand?"

She nodded.

"Does Missy still have the tape now?"

Again she silently affirmed.

"And from now on, Clara, when you listen to them, you will always use ear phones. Do you understand?"

"Yes, Tom." Her voice was a monotone.

"In a minute, I'm going to kiss you, Clara, and you'll forget that we had this conversation, but you will remember my instructions. Nod if you understand."

She did so.

"You will retain the suggestions not to lend your new tapes and to take your medication every night in your subconscious." He reinforced his instructions. "However, after I kiss you, you will resume your normal behavior."

Once he had glanced around the room, Tom pressed his lips to hers and then released her. "Come with me, Clara. I'll take you back by the punch table."

"Are you okay, honey?"

Missy heard the note of concern in her husband's voice when he sat down beside her after he had returned from his conversation with Sam. "I feel a little nauseous," she admitted.

"Maybe I should—Oh, Sam is dancing with Clara now."

"No, darling, don't bother Sam. I'm all right."

"Why don't I get you something to eat?" Alex offered and got up to get it.

While he was gone, Burt came by, stumbled against the table, and then sat in Alex's empty chair.

"I think you have the wrong table, Burt." Missy told him.

"S–s–sorry. Hey, how'd you like to c–come up to my room for whatever?" Burt stammered.

"Burt, of course not! I'm married. I'm Missy Marcus, the one you ran into today on the ski slope. Do you even remember that?"

"Oops." Burt stood and wobbled slightly. "Give you a couple of months." He waved his hand and staggered away. "Hey, Brenda!"

"To your left, Burt." Her high-pitched voice answered. "Keep coming."

"Missy, what's wrong?" Alex set his supplies down and sat beside her.

"Burt just dropped in by mistake. He asked me to go up to his room. I don't think he knew who I was. Then, when I told him, he said he would give us a couple of months! Alex, I don't want our marriage to go bad, ever."

"Sh." He leaned forward and touched his hand to her pale cheek. "Darling, that won't happen to us because we're committed to each other before the Lord, and we'll work together to preserve our love. We've been through so much already. And you know how much I truly love you, too." He drew his hand away to pick up his plastic fork. "I brought you some fruit salad and crackers along with the fruit punch."

She sampled the salad and nodded her approval. "Mm. Good. Thank you. I love you."

Alex's gaze caught Burt and Brenda as they walked toward the stairs together. Turning back to his wife he told her what he had witnessed and then he said thoughtfully. "You know, honey, we need to pray for Burt."

"Oh, Alex, why did you bring him up again?"

"Burt is really a lonely guy. That's why he acts the way he does, to get attention. Come on, honey, he needs our prayers too."

"Yeah, well, I just don't like him very much. He's just so obnoxious."

Alex sipped his punch. After replacing the glass, he responded, "Loneliness is painful. I know. Some people withdraw, and others become outspoken to compensate. Burt needs Jesus' love and forgiveness just as much as we do, Missy."

Missy sighed. "Why do I get the feeling you're trying to tell me something here?" A faint smile adorned her lips.

Alex chuckled audibly. Suddenly his expression changed to one of concern as he saw his wife's face grow paler and her smile fade into an open–mouth, wide–eyed stare.

Her hand grasped his firmly and she breathed the thought aloud in a whisper. "Alex, I think Burt reminds me of your college roommate, Arthur Wills."

Alex shook his head, not knowing what to say to her.

Her revelation was interrupted by Tom, whom neither of them had seen approaching their table. "Missy, are you all right? You look as if you've seen a ghost."

They both looked up in surprise.

Missy, who was still holding onto Alex's hand, began to stammer without really saying anything.

Then Alex spoke. "She's just feeling the after effects of her collision this morning. We didn't see you coming. Have a seat."

Tom shook his head. "No, thanks. I just wanted to let you know that I got the tape from Clara. I had wanted to borrow it. You know, the *Spiritual Gifts* tape you gave back to Clara tonight, Missy."

"Wait a minute, I haven't returned it yet," Missy answered. "She only gave it to me around lunchtime today."

"Well, I have it right here." Tom held up the case, and Alex recognized it. "You must have forgotten that you returned it."

Missy shook her head as Tom walked away. "Alex, I'm sure that I did not give it back to Clara. I forgot to bring it when we came down at suppertime."

"Do you want me to go and check our room?"

Missy shook her head and withdrew her hand from his. "Do

you see Clara anywhere around?"

Alex looked around, then answered. "She and Tom are over in the corner, talking rather closely together. Hey, Sam," Alex called in greeting.

Sam returned his friend's hail and headed for the Marcus's table. "What's up?" Sam asked when he was seated. "Hey, Missy, you look a bit peaked. Are you feeling all right?"

"Nice to have a professional opinion," Alex observed.

Missy shrugged.

Sam casually reached over to check her pulse at her wrist and then stood to examine the bump at the back of her head. Then he touched his hand to her forehead briefly before sitting down.

"Well?" Alex asked.

"It seems to be doing okay," Sam answered. "How do you feel, Missy?"

"I had a little nausea, and the headache still hasn't gone away. Sam, is it normal to be confused following a concussion?"

"It's not unusual," Sam answered. "A period of disorientation is to be expected. Other symptoms can include nausea, dizziness, and sometimes even memory loss, depending on the severity of the injury. These are usually temporary, though. Rest and time will help."

"Tom says that I returned a tape to Clara, but I don't remember doing it," Missy stated.

Sam shook his head. "Clara is a mystery all by herself."

Alex's grin did not go unnoticed by the other man.

"Alex, can you get Clara to come over here?" Missy asked.

"I'll see, Missy." He rose to leave the table and returned a few minutes later with the lady in question.

"Hello again, beautiful lady." Sam stood to hold a chair for Clara beside him.

"Hello, Sam, Missy."

"Clara, did I give you back your *Spiritual Gifts* tape? I'm sure I didn't. It should still be upstairs in my room."

"You gave it to me earlier this evening. Come now, you couldn't have forgotten already," Clara replied easily.

"But I couldn't have," Missy protested. "Alex, did you see me bring it down?"

"I really wasn't paying attention to what you were carrying, sweetheart," her husband said. "It doesn't matter, anyway. The important thing is that Clara has it back. Don't worry about it now."

"Clara, may I get you something to eat or drink?" Sam offered.

When she nodded, he rose to comply.

The conversation took on a lighter tone, but Missy couldn't forget the incident. She knew in her heart that she was right.

8
The Snow Ball Effect

Following warmup exercises the next morning, Doug Johnson repeated a previous safety speech, announced Burt's absence from the session, and wrapped up with the regrouping of ski partners. Teams of three were formed, with two students per instructor.

Alex quelled his wife's impetuousness by whispering to her. "Don't worry, honey, you and I will be paired together. I just know it."

Doug Johnson began to name off his groupings. "Alex and Missy Marcus with Sandy, Brenda and Marie with Ray, Clara and Tom with Sam—"

"Uh, excuse me, Doug," Clara interrupted him. "Why do I go with two sighted men?"

Doug patiently explained. "Sam will be instructing Tom on how to teach skiers who are blind by observing your technique. Tom has such talent for the sport, he would make an excellent instructor." Without waiting for further comments, he continued to divide up the remainder of the party into the designated groupings.

Alex was undecided whether he should attribute Tom's expression to a grin of triumph or a sneer of condescension. Either way, he knew that Clara was less than pleased with being the guinea pig. A faint smile tugged at the corners of his mouth as he encountered the gleam of excitement in Marie's eyes. He found himself momentarily envying her youthful exuberance. His expression sobered as his lack of self–confidence began to creep back over him. As the group started to move to get their gear, Alex reached for his wife's hand.

"Missy, I'm not very able at this yet."

"Don't worry, Alex," Sandy responded, "I'll keep you in line."

"Clara."

Sam's warm hand around hers helped to melt the chill that she had been feeling inside.

"Let's go." Tom's grip on her other hand was tighter, unrelenting. "Just think how skillful you'll be when we get through with you. Why, there is no telling what you'll be able to do."

Clara mumbled something that only Sam understood.

Sam tried to sound reassuring. "You're in good hands, I promise you."

The quiet calm and easy glide of the mountain slope provided a false sense of security as the morning sessions progressed without incident. Even Clara finally admitted to herself that she was enjoying the runs, not to mention the close attention being paid to her by two attractive males. When she stumbled and fell on the ascent, both guides rushed to her aid.

"Time to rest a while." Sam suggested. "Just a few more steps."

When they reached the top of the slope, Clara drew in a deep breath and then exhaled. "I love it here. It is so peaceful."

"You've never been in a blizzard?" Sam asked.

"Nor an avalanche?" Tom suggested.

Sam nodded knowingly.

"Ah, well, those things don't matter now," Clara replied with a sigh.

"No, but they could," Sam said quietly. "So, Tom, how do you like teaching?"

The taller man shrugged. "Piece of cake."

"Well, I like skiing," Clara asserted. "Let's go again."

Inside the lodge, Gloria Johnson had gone upstairs to knock on Burt's door, Number Fifteen, the room next to the newlyweds'.

"Who's there?" the male voice demanded from inside.

"It's Gloria Johnson, Doug's wife. It's almost time for lunch. Are you coming down?"

"In a few minutes," Burt answered.

She nodded silently and turned toward the staircase.

Burt appeared in the hallway while the members of the skiing party were removing outer clothing and putting equipment away.

"Hey, what was all the yelling about?" Burt asked.

"You missed it, Burt," Brenda retorted.

"Yeah, super fun," Marie added. "That was a great snowball fight. Plus, they even changed the rules, too."

Burt made a grunting noise and turned to lead the way to the dining room for lunch.

Alex and Missy claimed an unoccupied table. When they were seated, Missy turned to put her hand on her husband's arm. Then she gave him a brief kiss. "I had a wonderful time this morning. I'll never forget today. I love you."

He responded with an embrace.

"Quit acting like honeymooners, you two." Sam dragged

back a chair to sit down.

"Who's acting?" Alex retorted. He was still holding his bride. It was only seconds before they drew apart.

"I have to admit," Sam said, "it was scary snowball fighting while blindfolded, even if it was just for fun. I really can't imagine skiing downhill without knowing—" He paused momentarily. Then he continued. "It's been quite a while since I tried it once during my first orientation, when I started to teach here. Look at Clara, for example, who has never seen. She's amazing."

"You just trust and listen to your partner," Missy said.

"Missy, that sounds so simple, but it really isn't," Sam admitted. "Say, where is Clara, anyway?"

He and Alex looked around the room.

"Tom isn't here yet, either," Alex observed.

"Hi, everybody. Can I sit here?" Marie asked.

"Sure," Missy told her. "We have plenty of room."

"I guess we don't have to ask if you had fun this morning," Alex teased her.

The younger woman was already nodding vigorously. "Mm. I hope we can do that again, too." She looked up. "Huh, Sam?"

"Probably so," Sam said and nodded in agreement.

"I could be spoiled," Missy commented. "This food is delicious."

"Two weeks, and then it's over," Alex reminded her.

"Excuse me." Sam rose when he spotted Clara with her food tray. He went to guide her to their table and to the seat next to his. "We missed you," he told her.

"I had to go to the ladies' room," she answered without turning her head in his direction. Then she began to eat.

Marie swallowed her bite of food and then addressed her roommate. "Did you have fun today, Clara? I know I did."

Clara nodded.

"I'm ready for another snowball fight," Marie stated.

Alex thought Clara's behavior was odd as she set her fork down beside her plate and sat motionless. "Clara, eat your lunch," he suggested.

Obediently, she picked up her fork and resumed eating as before.

"What are you thinking about, Clara?" Sam asked her. "You're very quiet."

"Nothing," she replied.

"Alex, I still haven't seen Tom," Sam said.

Alex pointed. "He's over in the corner behind you, with the Johnsons and Ray."

"Alex, would you get me another dessert?" his wife asked him.

"What's this?" Sam teased.

Alex stood. "Anyone else want something?"

It became unanimous for more blueberry cobbler.

Missy smiled at her husband with gratitude when he returned. She knew his routine of taking his seizure medication during meals, which he considered to be a good habit and subtle reminder.

"Thank you, dear. I promise I'll work extra hard this afternoon to burn up calories," Missy vowed solemnly.

"Nice try," Sam chuckled.

"I don't mind eating seconds," Marie admitted.

Clara ate silently.

"Clara, you seem depressed. Are you okay?" Sam asked her.

"I'm fine." Clara answered. "I just want to finish so that we can go back outside. It's much nicer out there in the fresh, open air."

Alex nodded his agreement. "Same partners, Sam?"

The other man nodded.

When a hand squeezed Sam's shoulder, he glanced up and smiled.

"Staff meets before the run," Sandy told him briefly and then walked on.

"What are we in for now?" Missy speculated.

"Missy, you'd better finish up," Alex advised. "Most everyone else is finished, and they're heading out of the dining room."

His wife swallowed the remainder of her drink and then spoke. "Thanks for waiting for me. I'm ready now, Alex."

Leisure time passed quickly.

When Alex and Missy rejoined the others, who were gathering to put on their clothing, Marie was complaining to her instructor. "Of course ! I put them both right here," she protested and pointed to the spot.

"What's the matter, Marie?" Missy asked.

"We can't find my other ski pole. It doesn't make any sense. I know I put both of them right here, just like always."

"It doesn't seem to be here, Marie," Ray said. "Maybe we should check in your room just to be sure it isn't there."

"Go ahead, but I know it won't be there, either." Marie threw up her hands in frustration.

"Isn't it odd to lose just one ski pole?" her mother asked.

"Marie, you're becoming forgetful, like Missy."

"Clara!" Missy protested.

"Well, you forgot that you gave me back the tape," Clara said.

Missy stamped her foot into the ski boot and looked at her friend. "Yes, the tape, and that isn't the only odd th—"

"Missy, let me help you with your coat," Alex interrupted her.

The group waited expectantly as they heard the searchers descending the staircase.

"No luck," Ray reported. "Even Burt was speechless. Marie, you're sure you put them together?"

The blonde head nodded.

"I may know where to find someone who can help," Clara said.

"What do you mean?" Ray asked her.

As if summoned, Gloria Johnson approached the group from a different direction carrying the missing pole. "Anyone missing this?" she asked. "I found it in the ladies room, of all places. I know it didn't belong in there."

"How did it get there?" Marie exclaimed. Then she added her thanks. "I certainly didn't take it there. I know I didn't. I wouldn't leave it there, either."

"Well, never mind now. At least you have it back. Let's get started," Sandy suggested. "By the way, the more advanced group will be trying out the steeper slope and take the chair lift to come back up."

"Oh, no, not me," Clara spoke up quickly. "I don't want to use that thing. I want to keep both of my feet on the ground."

"Don't be afraid Clara." Sam put his arm around her shoulders reassuringly. "One of us will be with you at all times."

"Now, Clara, that's what you said about flying, too. Remember?" Tom reminded her. "Don't underestimate yourself."

"I'm with Clara," Missy admitted. "I never thought I'd fly in a plane, either, but, well, we are here, aren't we?" She looked to her husband for reassurance.

"You never know what you're capable of until you're

tested," Alex said, and then he added softly, "There is God–given strength in weakness. I can testify to that."

Missy smiled and said, "Trust your partner, Clara. You'll be all right."

The dark–haired woman shook her head. "I don't know. My horoscope said today to keep both feet firmly on the ground and keep your eyes looking forward to the future."

Tom chuckled and then said, "It looks as if you're wrong on both counts, Clara. I told you that stuff was for the loonies."

Clara's chin lifted. "I don't believe everything you say to me, Tom." Defiance edged her voice.

"As I said," Sandy repeated, "let's get going, shall we?"

Following the afternoon session, Alex and Missy returned to their room to rest before it was time for supper. Alex sat on the edge of the bed to remove his shoes and then stretched out languidly on the bed. He then reached easily across to pull his bride down beside him. "Relax a while, honey."

"I'm too excited," she replied. She sat upright with her back leaning against the headboard. She could see that he was smiling up at her. The corners of her mouth turned upward automatically.

Alex reached up to pick a strand of long brown hair and jiggle it gently. "You know, Mrs. Marcus, this trip was a wonderful idea."

She nodded and then spoke gleefully, "Yes, and who didn't want to go, at first? Who persuaded whom that we would have a good time?"

"Yeah, I know. Although I do also remember someone who really didn't want to go up in an airplane, either. I do have to admit, though, that I've surprised myself. You know I have trouble with my balance sometimes."

"Yes, darling, but you haven't had a seizure for almost a year, now," she reminded him.

"No, I haven't. You're right. Finally got a medication that works. I take it properly and see the doctor regularly, anyway."

"Yes," she agreed absently. After a moment, she spoke again. "Alex, thinking of doctors and medications, I was thinking about Clara's behavior."

He had dropped her hair, and now his voice took on a more serious note. "Missy, I think we should keep our speculations to ourselves as much as possible. That's why I stopped you earlier, when Marie had lost her ski pole. Be careful what you reveal."

She nodded. "I know. Hold my tongue. I didn't think."

He nodded in turn, and she poked his side, causing him to jump unexpectedly.

"I can't get any straight answers from Tom," Alex told her. "I've asked him for the name of Clara's doctor, but he keeps avoiding my questions. I didn't want to put Clara on the defensive or have her thinking that we just wanted to be nosy. You know what I'm trying to say."

"Yes," she agreed.

"I'm beginning to think that Sam is the only one around here who has his head on straight," Alex mused.

Rapping at their room door interrupted their conversation. It was followed shortly by Clara's high calling, "Missy, Alex, are you there? Please, I must talk to you." She continued to knock.

Alex went quickly to the door to open it. Taking her hand, he led Clara inside and queried her about the cause of her anxiety. While guiding her, he picked up a desk chair and set it beside the bed. Once she was seated on the chair, he sat on the edge of the bed beside his wife.

"Take it easy, Clara," Missy tried to comfort her friend.

"You're safe here. Calm down and tell us what's wrong."

After a few moments Clara was composed enough to speak. "I just had to talk to someone. I know that you don't like this, but my horoscope...There's death in my future!"

"Clara, what in the world are you saying?" Missy's bewilderment was evident in her tone.

"What do you mean Clara?" Alex asked.

"The Card of Death. Someone who's close to me is going to die! I drew the Card of Death!" She began to sob again and her words were choppy. "I do not know who or when, but it will be soon. The cards don't lie."

"Whose cards?" Alex asked her.

"Mrs.—Uh, my friend, who's a fortune teller, she told me. She read it in the cards. She did not want to tell me, but I made her."

"Don't worry about things that you can't control," Missy advised. "Surely you're not going to murder someone, Clara."

"But why?" Clara asked.

"You don't have to worry about some vague prediction," Alex explained to her. "There are no facts or evidence to prove this theory, right?"

Clara shook her head and then said, "But the cards don't lie."

Alex sighed and then said, "All right, then, Clara, since you have a premonition about disaster happening, maybe it can be avoided. If we all are aware, and if we're extra safety conscious, maybe it won't happen."

"Do you think so?" She raised large, dark eyes in his direction.

"Clara, have you told this to your doctor in New York?" Missy ventured.

The other woman shook her head. "No. When I couldn't

reach Dr. Sorenson by telephone, I came straight here to see you two. I just had to talk to someone. You understand?"

Alex touched her clenched hands. "Of course we do, Clara. Now, don't let this upset you any further. Remember, we're going to try to avoid this incident if we can. Maybe we can prevent it from ever happening."

"Oh, I hope so! Thank you, both of you."

"You may come to see us any time, Clara," Missy offered. "We want to help, and we're your friends. You can trust us."

"It's almost time for supper," Alex reminded them. "Shall we go?"

Missy chuckled as she bounced off the bed.

That evenings events included an old-fashioned sleigh ride, and then inside, Brenda played piano for a sing-along. Gloria Johnson served hot chocolate and brownies.

Alex and Missy were sitting on the couch enjoying their semiprivate intimacy.

"Gosh, Missy, I haven't done this since my brother, Ben, and I were kids and Mom was still alive. She made the smoothest hot chocolate." He concentrated his gaze on his cup.

"A perfect evening," Missy observed. "Perfect because I'm sharing it with you. I love you, Alex Marcus."

He nodded. Then he set his cup down and took her hand. Lifting it to his lips, he then released it. When his gaze rose he spoke hastily. "Burt, be careful! Missy is sitting here with me. There's an empty chair behind you."

"Okay, thanks." The other man slumped into an easy chair near the couch.

"Having a good time tonight, Burt?" Missy asked cordially.

Burt shrugged his shoulders. "No big deal. I'll tell ya,

though, this hot chocolate could use a kick."

"Well, you must like Brenda's music, at least?"

A sly grin answered Alex's question. "You betcha."

"Burt, aren't you enjoying the skiing lessons?" Missy asked.

"Too restrictive."

"We have to start somewhere," Missy countered.

Burt grunted. "I'd like another brownie."

"Here you are." Alex took one from the plate with a napkin and handed it to Burt.

"Me, too." Missy reached down to take another.

"Sam misses a lot of fun," Alex commented. "I don't think I'd like working second shift. I like to have my nights free."

Burt chuckled. "Now, that I can agree with, man. Variety is it."

"No, Burt, I don't agree with you at all, there," Alex said.

"Oh, you will in time," Burt retorted. "All men like it that way. They just don't want to admit to it, that's all."

Missy stood. "If you two will excuse me, I'm going to find Clara."

"Truth hurts," Burt said.

"Never mind, Missy," Alex said quickly. "You know I love only you, and I'm proud to have you as my wife."

Burt sighed as if bored.

Alex stood to give his bride a kiss.

She smiled up at him and then turned to go find her friend.

When he resumed his seat, Alex spoke to the other man. "Wait until you meet the woman of your dreams, Burt. That will make all the difference. You'll see what I am talking about then."

Burt shook his head. "Woman was made to serve man. That's life, Alex. Get what you can while you can. That's what I say."

"I don't agree with you at all."

"Your choice, pal. But I know what I'm talking about."

"Well, Burt, you'll have to excuse me. I have to make a phone call." Alex rose. "See you later."

Alex left the open lobby behind and walked down the hall to use the pay telephone there. After removing the receiver, he inserted his change and then dialed the directory for New York State information. He was facing the instrument on the wall and didn't notice an approaching shadow behind him. The narrow area was quiet and dimly lit.

He spoke clearly into the mouthpiece. "For the Dream Research Department," he said. "I'd like the number to reach Dr. Sorenson." Obediently, he spelled the name. Following a pause, he entrusted the receiver to his right hand and wrote on a small note pad he had laid inside the receptacle. As he replaced the receiver, the shadow withdrew quickly and quietly.

The next morning, when Alex returned to their table, Missy was still eating breakfast alone. "No luck," he told her upon resuming his seat. "I couldn't get through to this Dr. Sorenson. They gave me the usual runaround."

His bride nodded. "At least you tried. You can try again later, honey."

"Alex, I need to talk to you." Sam set down his tray and pulled out a chair.

"Want me to leave?" Missy asked. "This sounds urgent."

"No, Missy, I just don't want this to get around to the other guests. And, yes, it is urgent." Sam paused to take a gulp of his decaf coffee. Then he continued in a lower tone. "One of our personnel files is missing. They're kept in a locked cabinet in the infirmary. I was checking through them this morning. That's when I noticed it."

"Doug knows?"

Sam nodded in response to Alex's question. "If you're wondering why I'm telling you this, it's your file that's missing, Alex."

Missy drew in her breath audibly.

"Is anyone missing a key?" Alex asked.

"Not that I know about," Sam replied.

"Maybe it's just accidentally misfiled or misplaced?" Missy asked, with a hopeful rise in the pitch of her voice.

"I hope so, but I checked and rechecked and will again after breakfast," Sam told her.

Then Missy asked, "Is anyone missing from the group?"

Both of her male companions looked around the room.

"Not that I can see, honey," her husband replied. "Tom is the last one in line for breakfast. No, Burt's behind him. What's going on around here, anyway?"

"I wish I knew," Sam said.

"It seems as if Clara's problems are having a snowball effect."

"What do you mean, Alex?" his wife asked him.

"I mean," Alex explained, "it seems that what has started out as one person's little idiosyncrasy has snowballed to affect more of us progressively, on a larger scale than we could have ever imagined, and it's still continuing."

"In other words," Sam added, "one small problem has grown to encompass much larger ones and pulled all of us into the snowball effect."

9
Something Sinister

Sam was as glad for the ski lesson to spend time with Clara as he was for the diversion from his worries. There was no good reason for Alex's epileptic condition to become general knowledge. The rest of the files had to be protected. Brenda, for example, was diabetic. He sighed and tried to concentrate his attention on Clara's progress.

"Sam," Clara breathed his name as she approached him, "how about a break?"

His genuine smile was audible in his voice. "Yes, of course." He took her gloved hands in his, causing her ski poles to dangle from the straps over her wrists. "Ah, Clara, you are as graceful as a falling snow flake."

Then his warm lips were on hers, gently drawing her into his closeness. Caught off guard, she had no time to shield herself from her own emotions.

Her true response sparked a hope in Sam, and a still unconscious resolve to win her heart began to kindle. Gently, he released her and stood back.

Fearing vulnerability, Clara swallowed and spoke

impulsively. "Surely that's not part of the regular lesson. Or is it?"

It took a moment for the implication of her words to have an impact on him. "Oh, no, Clara, believe me, I've never—It's just that you, uh, have this effect on me. I never know how you're going to react. Clara, I'll never kiss you again unless you ask me to, okay?"

"Don't forget it," she said, but her face was bent toward the ground.

"Ready to ski some more?" he asked.

"Yes," she responded meekly.

Upon returning to the lodge, Clara asked Sam to tell Missy that she wanted to speak with her. He relayed the message when he found Missy in her husband's arms in a far corner of the recreation room.

"Sam, any news?" Alex asked while he still held his new wife.

Sam shook his head. "I'll let you know when there is." Then he left.

"Happy?" Alex spoke in a low voice and then covered her lips with his own before she could answer him.

When she was able to speak, Missy said, "Keep this up, and we could very well miss lunch." She withdrew her hands from behind his neck to shield his advance.

Impulsively, he moved his hands to tickle her sides, and delighted in her squeal. She grabbed his hands to restrain him and said, "In spite of everything, I couldn't have dreamed of a more perfect honeymoon. Now, darling, I'm going to see what Clara wants." She released his hands and turned to go.

"Missy, be careful," he warned her. "I hope it isn't something sinister." The latter was spoken without forethought.

Surprise caused her to turn back around. "Alexander

Marcus, whatever do you mean by that?"

He shook his head and repeated. "Just be careful."

She nodded and left him alone.

When they were alone in the ladies' room, Clara confided to Missy about Sam's behavior that morning and her resulting confusion.

"Normal," Missy responded.

"How can you say normal?" her friend asked. "If so-called love makes you be confused, that's no fun."

"It only seems that way for a while," Missy tried to explain. "You think that you want to hate the guy but you're drawn to him, attracted to and aware of everything about him. Clara, you don't have to be afraid. Let yourself feel, but be honest with yourself, too."

"But why do I feel this way about Sam? I know that I ha—" Catching herself, she closed her mouth.

Missy tried to encourage her to finish the statement. "What were you going to say, Clara?"

After a moment, Clara revised her sentence. "I mean that I know how I feel about Tom. There's no question about that."

"Does Tom like you too?" Missy asked her.

"It's hard to explain sometimes, Missy. I don't know, exactly. Sometimes he scares me."

Missy put her hand on Clara's arm. "Any time you need help, you can come to me and Alex. And Sam, too, I'm sure. Remember that."

The other woman nodded. "Thank you, Missy. I do need a friend."

"We are your friends, Clara, and we want to help in any way we can."

"I know. We should go eat now. We'll be missed, I think." Clara responded.

Alex went to assist the ladies to his table when he saw them in the food line at last. "I thought you two weren't coming," he joked after they were settled.

"Very funny," Missy retorted. "Have you seen Sam?"

"Nope," he replied and took a bite of meat.

"Enjoying your skiing lessons?" Clara asked.

"Mm," Missy answered quickly. "It's great. Perfect."

"No such thing as perfect," Clara countered.

"Aren't you enjoying yourself, Clara?" Alex asked her.

Clara nodded. "That's not what I meant. You know the saying about being too happy, and then something happens to spoil it all."

Missy replaced her tea cup audibly. "Don't say that. Don't even think that way, please."

"Well, I don't suppose you ladies would mind sharing the discussion you had earlier?" Alex was trying to change the direction of the conversation.

Clara shook her head silently.

"Men," Missy said simply.

"On that note, I think I'll go back for seconds." Alex stood to go take his medication and then pick up an extra dessert.

During his absence, Sam arrived with his tray to join the women.

"You did almost miss lunch," Missy told him.

"Where have you been, Sam?" Clara asked.

"I took Tom into town so he could pick up a special delivery package that came for him. I know the area, so it was quicker that way," Sam explained. "Where's Alex?" Sam gulped his black coffee and began to eat.

"He'll be right back," Missy said. "I hope he remembers my extra dessert."

"Sometimes I think I'm going out of my mind," Sam said.

Clara choked slightly on her bread.

"What happened now?" Missy asked. Absently she picked up her tea cup, but replaced it again when she realized it was empty.

"I found the missing file. It was just misplaced, after all, it seems. I had gone back to the infirmary to check again after this morning's lessons. Alex's file was in another drawer."

"You must be relieved," Missy said, expressing her own feelings.

Sam nodded.

"Anything else missing?" Missy asked him.

"No. It just doesn't make sense."

Alex returned, to Missy's delight, with another cup of tea and their chocolate cream pies. He greeted Sam, and Sam, in turn, related his story to Alex.

"I just saw Tom," Alex told them when Sam had finished speaking, "and he wasn't very congenial. He seemed to be in kind of a hurry."

"Probably because he almost missed lunch," Clara observed.

"Oh, by the way, Clara," Sam began, "since Tom is one of our most accomplished skiers, I'm going to let him be your guide for this afternoon's session. Okay?"

"Where are you going?" she asked.

"Nowhere. I'll be watching."

"Clara, if you'd rather not—"

"Melissa," Alex reprimanded.

"No problem," Clara answered.

"Hello, folks." Tom stood facing their table.

"Have a seat," Alex offered amiably.

Tom did. He speared his meat and asked, "Did Sam tell you the good news, Clara?"

She nodded.

Missy turned toward her husband and said, "I think it's great having your own personal ski partner. I love mine."

"Yes, it's almost as good as having your own dance partner," Clara observed. "I can't decide which I like better."

"That depends on your partner." Tom shot a glance in Sam's direction then he turned his attention back to Clara. "Wait and see my Little Rose."

Missy wriggled in her chair, trying silently to erase John 10:10 from her mind.

"Something wrong, honey?"

"I'm so full Alex. Could we walk?"

"Sure. Will you people excuse us?" He rose and held the chair for his lady.

He led her to the supply area to get their coats and boots, and then they went outside and around to the front porch. When they had stopped walking, he queried her. "Now what is this all about? Somehow I don't believe it's just to be alone with me. Although..." He let his voice trail off.

"Alex, I need to tell you what Clara said to me. And don't you think it's odd that Sam found your file after it had been missing for a period of time? I don't believe it was simply misplaced. And why *your* file, Alex?" She took in a breath and then continued after breathing out. "You know, Clara is afraid of Tom. You know I don't trust him, either. I can't help it. He reminds me of Arthur Wills."

"Calm down, Missy." He began to stroke her hair with his gloved hand. "I think you are making much to do about nothing."

Ignoring his remark she then asked, "Have you noticed the sparks between Clara and Sam?"

"Actually, I've been too busy noticing you, darling."

She moved slightly to avoid his kiss. "Alex, be serious. No, not that way." She found herself in his embrace. She was unable to hide the delight in her voice. "It won't work, not this time. You're not going to take my mind off the subject."

"What is the subject?" His lips brushed her neck.

"You could be in danger, Alex. Be serious about this, please."

He sighed and released his hold. "I thought we were concerned about Clara. Remember?"

She nodded. "Have you gotten to talk to her doctor in New York yet? I wonder, too, what this important package thing is about. You can bet Tom won't tell us."

"Why should he? And no to your other question. I keep leaving messages for Dr. Sorenson. He's always busy when I call, and he hasn't returned one of my calls yet."

"Tom seems to be pretty possessive where Clara is concerned. He's only a lab technician, not her doctor," Missy protested.

"But he does have to protect a client's right to privacy."

"Yeah, you're right," Missy agreed.

Alex bent his head so his face was close to hers. "Missy, try to forget about the past and give Tom the benefit of the doubt." His kiss was brief and she lifted her head slightly for another.

"I love you sweetheart," she whispered afterward.

Silently, Alex thanked his Lord for the happiness that he felt with his new wife.

They were walking through the lobby when Doug's wife passed them on her way upstairs.

"Beware," she muttered, "evil is among us. It will destroy."

"How does she know?" Missy asked.

"I know." The answer came from the steps.

Alex ushered her forward in silence. In the hallway he stopped and spoke. "Missy, I'm going to call Pete. Maybe he can be of some help."

Missy's expression brightened. She waited while her husband made the phone call. Newspaperman Peter Early, Alex's best friend from college, had assisted in the initial investigation that had revealed the background information on Clarissa Méndez two and a half years earlier. Missy was sure that Early Bird Pete could dig up just about any kind of information.

Once Alex had hung up the phone, she asked, "So, how is the Early Bird?"

Alex chuckled softly and assured her of Pete's assistance. "Pete is going to try to interview Dr. Sorenson," Alex told her. "If anyone can get through to Dr. Sorenson, Pete will."

She nodded and hugged his arm.

"Let's get back before we miss the afternoon session," he said. "I need lots of practice."

Prior to the afternoon session, Doug had called everyone, staff and guests, to assemble in the recreation room for a reiteration of his safety lecture. There was an additional discussion on privacy, security, and entry into unauthorized sectors of the building. Alex and Missy had arrived soon after this part of the discussion had begun. Once Burt had promised, on his honor, to be on his most obedient behavior, he was allowed to rejoin the ski party.

"I love it," Missy declared. She and Alex were preparing to go downstairs for supper that evening.

Alex embraced her. "What?" he asked as he held her close to him.

She looked up into his face and smiled for a moment. Then she replied. "I love skiing, and I love spending all this time with you. I wish we could be on our honeymoon forever. I don't want it to end, Alex."

"It doesn't have to end."

She asked him to repeat.

"I said it doesn't have to end. The feeling, I mean." He touched his lips to her forehead gently. "As long as we keep loving each other, it will never end."

She made a little gasp of excitement and tightened her embrace momentarily. "You mean, like loving God with all your heart and mind and soul. I see. You mean, put your heart into it!"

Her lips earnestly sought his and were rewarded immediately. Afterward she rested her cheek against the wool sweater that was covering his shoulder. Sighing, she reminded him that it was time to go downstairs.

"Some day," Alex promised, "we're going to finish this at the same time we start, with no interruptions."

Missy chuckled and then said, "We have a lifetime, sweetheart. Are you ready to go?"

"I suppose so." He went to open the door and almost ran into Burt, who had just come out of the room next door. "Sorry Burt," Alex apologized quickly. "I didn't see you coming."

"Didn't see you, either," Burt replied and kept on walking.

Missy grunted. "He seems cheerful this evening."

"See, anything is possible," Alex commented.

"That's what I'm afraid of."

Marie waved on her way downstairs, and Alex waved back, as well as speaking a pleasant greeting to her.

"Sam isn't here, is he?" Missy asked.

"No, he's gone to work," Alex reminded her.

"I just thought to check to make sure nothing else is missing."

"Missy, you worry too much. Besides, you can ask Doug,"

Alex told her.

"Of course. That's right. Why didn't I think of that?" she asked.

"Because you were thinking of worrying," he teased.

She pretended to poke at him.

Alex and Missy were sitting by themselves, eating, when Tom stepped over to their table. "Excuse me," he barked.

They both looked up and Alex gestured for Tom to join them.

He set his tray down with a clatter and sat down. "Have either of you seen Clara?"

They shook their heads. Missy said, "I haven't seen her since the last ski session this afternoon."

"Come to think of it," Alex added, "she wasn't with Marie when she came down, either."

Tom replaced his coffee cup on the tray. "I've already spoken to Marie, and she hasn't seen Clara either. I'm worried. She tends to be—" he hesitated for emphasis "—a little unstable at times."

"Care to elaborate?" Alex seized the opening.

Tom shrugged but said nothing more.

Missy looked at Tom and said, "We want to help Clara in any way we can."

"She has trouble separating fantasy from reality. You don't know her circumstances. So the best thing you can do for her is stay out of it."

"But, she's a friend, and—"

"Missy," her husband interrupted her quickly, "Tom has a point." He wished she could see well enough to read his expression.

"But, Alex," she protested.

"Eat your supper, honey," He advised. Under the table he

moved his foot to lightly tap the toe of her shoe. Then as he glanced around the room, he saw Clara in line waiting to be served. "Here's Clara now," he exclaimed. "She's getting her food."

Almost before Alex had finished speaking, Tom rose from his chair to guide Clara to the table. On the way back, he walked slowly and seemed to be talking intently to her, Alex noted. While he had the opportunity, he whispered clearly to his wife to be careful what she said around Tom.

"Clara, we missed you," Alex said to her when she had been seated across from Tom and beside Missy.

"I was talking and forgot the time," Clara offered.

"Talking to whom?" Missy asked without thinking.

"I'd rather not say," Clara stated.

Tom put his coffee cup down with noticeable emphasis. He made a noise as if clearing his throat and said, "I told you not to fool around with that horoscope stuff. You have enough problems without making more trouble."

"I'm not making the trouble," Clara responded. "Something sinister is going to happen. It has been predicted, and I can feel it."

"Clara, you're scaring me," Missy said.

"What do you mean?" Alex asked. "Can you explain it further?"

Clara shook her head. "I don't know. It is just that Glo—" She stopped, realizing that she had almost revealed the name of the person she was trying to protect. "It has been predicted. That's all that I know."

"Do you know why or how?" Alex persisted.

"No."

"It's no use trying to make sense out of superstition," Tom said. "I've told her before to stay away from that stuff. Haven't I,

Clara?" After a pause he asked, "Are you still taking your sleeping medication like you're supposed to?"

"Yes, Tom," she answered promptly.

Tom sighed and decided to change the subject before Alex could ask any more questions. "So, what's on the agenda for tonight?"

"Hey, aint ya heard?" Burt yelled. "It's a square dance, and I hope they serve something better than ginger ale, too."

"Oh, boy," Alex groaned.

Tom chuckled. He misinterpreted Alex's reaction as a reflection on Burt's behavior.

"We've never been to a square dance," Missy explained. She knew that her husband was not keen on activities that depended upon good balance.

"Well, there's always a first time for everything," Tom commented. Then he asked, "You two are coming, aren't you?"

"I don't know," Alex answered, hoping to drop the subject.

"Oh, come on," Clara encouraged. "It will be fun. You'll see."

"Clara, do you know how to do it?" Missy asked.

Her friend nodded.

"Sounds as if we would really be missed if we didn't go," Missy pleaded.

"I don't feel like talking about it," Alex said. "I'm going to get some more tea. Anyone else want something?"

"Another dessert, please, and tea," his wife said.

"I'd like another salad," Clara added.

Once everyone was settled following Alex's trip back to the food area, Tom was the first one to speak. "Tell you what, Alex, if you and Missy go to the dance tonight, I'll have a talk with you afterward about the subject we were discussing earlier. Okay? Is that a deal?"

Alex frowned momentarily and then made a sound of

surprise. Finally he agreed. "I guess so." He sipped his tea and continued to eat in silence.

Once they had finished eating and gone upstairs, leaving Tom and Clara alone, Missy asked her husband, "You really don't want to go tonight, do you?"

"Not really," he admitted. He sat on the edge of the bed to remove his shoes and then stretched out on his back, locking his hands behind his head. "Tom surprised me," he said half to himself. "I wasn't expecting to be bribed into going."

"That was an odd thing for him to say, wasn't it?"

"Yeah. And Clara's behavior—well, I guess it's normal for her to act abnormal."

Missy, who had removed her shoes and socks, moved closer to his side. "Astrology can be dangerous if misused." She began to stroke his forehead with a light touch.

"Too many problems," he said quietly.

"It's too soon for Pete to call you back, I guess." She brushed his wavy locks backward, messing up his hair.

He sighed. "Why do people act the way they do?" Then a slight chuckle, and he pulled his hands out from behind his head. "I'm supposed to be the psychologist. Missy—"

He had turned on his side, and her lips were on his. She was determined to bring him out of his sullen mood.

"Oh, Missy," he murmured, and his kisses became more frequent.

"I love you, Alex," she whispered in his ear.

Soon they were under the covers, fulfilling their roles as husband and wife. This time, no music played and no sound interrupted or added any artificiality to their lovemaking.

Afterward, they lay in contented silence. Finally, Missy asked, "Are you feeling better now, love?"

He murmured and moved to touch her forehead with his

cheek. He was otherwise snugly close to his bride. After a moment, he said to her, "Neither one of us is moving from here until we leave to go home."

"Now, Alex." She tried to scold but her voice was gleeful. Then she added, "No, neither one of us could go that long without food."

"Mm." His lips were caressing hers again.

Still later, she remarked, "It must be time to go back downstairs."

"Why?" he asked innocently.

"The square dance we agreed to attend," she reminded him.

He sighed and rolled onto his back, releasing her.

Following a shower and a discussion of appropriate apparel, they were finally ready to depart. Alex locked the door to their room, Number Eleven, and they proceeded down to the cafeteria, where the floor had been cleared for the gala. They stood just inside the doorway, holding hands, politely waiting for the current dance to finish before venturing further inside.

The caller announced a fifteen–minute break for refreshments. Alex took this as his cue.

"Sounds great to me." Burt's comment could be heard throughout the large room.

Tom cleared his throat and greeted them with, "A little late, aren't we?"

Alex returned his grin with a twinkle in his eyes. His erect posture with shoulders back was meant to display the air of a satisfied man. Turning to his wife he asked, "Punch or tea?"

After a moment she replied, "Plain punch."

He nodded and complied.

"Aw, that's no fun." Burt slurred his words as he stumbled toward them. Then he jibed, "And what have we been doing all this time?"

"What do you think, Burt?" Alex countered.

"Missy, Alex, hello." Clara had followed the sound of their voices.

"Hi, Clara." Missy greeted her friend heartily. She was grateful for the diversion. "Are you enjoying yourself?"

"Naturally," Tom answered.

"Clara?" Missy asked again.

The lady nodded and replied affirmatively. "You'll enjoy it, too. Wait until the next dance."

"Professionals and all." Alex noted the men in fancy Western duds. "Catered, too."

"Nice, huh?" Clara observed.

Again Burt's bawl cut loose. "Aw, come on, gimme a bigger glass 'n this fing. I'm real thirsty."

Alex began another conversation. "Well, Clara, I guess you feel relieved now that nothing bad has happened. Maybe you'll believe that horoscope prediction isn't real, after all."

Clara shook her head vigorously. "It didn't say when the evil would manifest itself, remember, just that it would."

"Now, Clara," Tom objected, "I thought we had agreed that you wouldn't get carried away with this stuff anymore." His gaze was intent upon her.

"You agreed, not I," she responded.

"Excuse me," Tom said. "I'd like to ask Marie to promenade. She's quite a good dancer." He got up to leave the small gathering.

"Sometimes he's too bossy," Clara commented when she thought Tom had gone out of their range of hearing.

"Does he still scare you?" Missy asked directly.

"Sometimes."

"Missy, I see someone I need to speak with," Alex told her

quickly. "I'll be back shortly."

Before his wife could ask who it was, he was gone.

"Hello, Gloria," Alex greeted his hostess.

"Good to see you, Alex."

"How long have you been practicing astrology?" he asked.

Her eyebrows rose slightly, but she responded with a question. "Who told you that?"

"No one. I just inferred it from various conversations."

"Really?"

He nodded, still confident.

"What does it matter?"

"It matters when it affects people who are vulnerable to it." Not wanting to stay on the defensive, Alex plunged ahead. "I want to know exactly what you said to Clara about something evil that's supposed to take place. Something sinister, I think it was."

"Ah, Clara."

Alex shook his head quickly. "No. I told you. No one said anything to me directly. There have been times, I've noticed, when both you and Clara have been missing from the group, and I just put the two together, so to speak. Now, about my question."

"You're very observant. I told her nothing," Gloria replied. "She drew the Card of Death. I have no control over the cards."

"How did you get her mixed up in this stuff, anyway?"

"You're mistaken. It was she who approached me."

"But you knew she was pliable?"

"Her interest didn't begin here, if that's what you're implying. I have already said, it was she who came to me." Following a slight silence, she added, "I am just a medium."

"You know that Clara is highly susceptible."

"Some people are more in tune to the spirit world." She

looked away, and, after another small silence, she added, "Alex, there's no need to mention this to Doug, is there?"

After thinking over the implication of this, he replied, "Not unless it becomes necessary." Then he turned and walked away without giving her time to respond.

Just as Alex returned with his and Missy's punch, the caller announced, "Grab your partner and let's go!"

"Where's Tom?" Clara asked.

"I don't see him," Alex told her.

"Come with me, Alex. I'll show you what to do," Clara offered.

Missy nodded and smiled at her friend's eagerness as Alex was pulled into the line with Clara.

"How 'bout it?"

Missy recognized Ray's voice and extended her hand to him to be led onto the floor.

Then Doug danced with Clara. After several partner changes, Alex was finally paired up with Missy and they danced together. Excitement heightened during the free fast-moving American tradition.

During one of the breaks, Burt had stumbled his way through the guests, announcing his loud good nights. When he finally reached the doorway, everyone else chimed in a chorus, "Good night, Burt!" Giggles and laughter followed all around.

At the second-floor landing, Burt turned right to follow the wall to his room. His cane tapped, bumped against a wooden echo as air prickled his cheek indicating open space. The door had opened slightly when his cane had collided with it.

Here already, he thought.

He stepped into the room, pushing the door open even further with the size of his body.

With his dulled senses, he was unaware at first of the slight sound. Once he became aware of the rattling sound, he followed it.

"Hey, what's 'a matta with the door?"

He fumbled with the bathroom door knob and finally got it open. As he turned the knob, a clattering of clicking sounds met his ears. Several steps into the small room, Burt recognized breathing as an indication of another presence. His mouth began to open to form the question when the swift blow felled him, after which he would wonder no more.

"Sorry, Burt. You're not my keeper."

Gloved hands hurried now to finish scooping the rest of the pills into the plastic bottle. The bottle was left lying on the counter on its side while the murderer fled the room, closing the door to Number Eleven behind.

10
A Brush with the Truth

"Alex, wasn't that fun?" Missy asked breathlessly as she and her husband were climbing the stairs to their room later that evening. "You were great!"

"Aren't you just a little prejudiced?" he asked.

She reached up to pat his shoulder lightly.

Alex smiled as he reached into his back pants pocket for the room key ring. He unlocked the door to room Number Eleven and they went inside.

"We should sleep well tonight," Missy commented.

They both walked to the bed to sit and remove shoes. Missy dropped her slip on shoes and then looked around. Her groom was standing, not moving.

"Alex." She spoke in a clear, distinct tone, fearing the onset of a seizure.

His hand came up and he said, "Stay there."

Slowly he walked toward the open bathroom door. Without turning, he spoke. "Go see if Sam's back and bring Doug, too. Right away."

"Alex, what's the matter?" She reached for her shoes.

"Just do it quickly." Glancing at her back he called, "Shut the door, but don't lock it."

A few minutes later she returned with both men.

"We haven't touched anything except the door knob," Alex reported upon their arrival. "I found him exactly as is."

"Him?" Missy stepped closer and saw the body for the first time. She put one hand over her mouth and slipped the other around her husband's arm.

"Burt's dead," Sam reported after a quick examination of the body.

"That pill bottle dumped over on the counter concerns me," Alex said. "I can't see the label."

"Don't touch it," Sam advised. "This is going to be a long night, I'm afraid."

"I'll go call the police," Doug stated and left the room.

"Burt's dead," Missy repeated.

"It looks as if he fell and hit his head," Sam observed.

"What was he doing in our room?" Missy asked.

"We don't know," Alex said. Then he added an afterthought. "Maybe he was in the wrong room by mistake."

"What was his room number?" Missy asked.

"Fifteen," Sam supplied. "The next room after yours. What time did Burt leave the dance, and what condition was he in at that time?"

Alex answered, "He was quite drunk. In fact, we all called good night to him because he interrupted so many people while he was trying to find his way out of the room. I didn't pay any attention to the time."

"How could he get into our room by mistake?" Missy asked. "It was locked, remember, Alex?"

He nodded. "It looks as if he wanted to take something for a head ache or hangover." Alex looked around the room. "Nothing else seems to be disturbed. That's odd. If he thought he was in his own room..." Alex shrugged.

Sam sat on one of the desk chairs. "The police will sort it out. Don't worry."

Alex walked over to the other desk chair and seated his wife after he had angled the chair to face away from the open bathroom door.

"I'm okay," she told him. "I've seen a dead body before."

He nodded briefly. Then he said, "I want to talk to Sam."

The two men converged on the scene in the bathroom. The body lay facing up with one section of the collapsible cane across its neck. No marks appeared to mar the front. Nor did the angle of the body indicate any outward signs of a struggle.

"Could he have overdosed on those pills?" Alex wondered.

"Not likely, given the state he was in," Sam said. "But to fall and hit his head hard enough to kill himself?" Sam shook his head.

"It appears that nothing else has been disturbed," Alex said.

Sam nodded. "We'll know more soon."

Following the questions by the police, it was determined that Alex and Missy would sleep in Burt's room for the time being. This would be temporary while the body was removed and evidence was collected for analysis.

"We'll be okay, honey," Alex tried to reassure her when they finally got into bed.

"I have some questions of my own that I'd like answered," she told him.

"I know, but tomorrow is another day."

"Yeah." It was a sigh more than a word.

"Sleep well, sweetheart." Alex turned on his side.

Sometimes the barrier between reality and the subconscious seems insurmountable. Finally Alex managed to rouse his wife from her nightmare.

"Just a bad dream." He held and soothed her in his arms.

"I dreamed that Clara was arrested for Burt's murder," She confessed to his shoulder.

"But the police are convinced that it was just an accidental fall," he reminded her.

"Hmph," she grunted.

"Anyway, it's time to get dressed for breakfast."

She raised her head but still held him in her embrace. "Already? I feel as if I haven't slept at all."

He kissed her. "You'll feel better once we get back into the normal routine. I imagine that Doug will make some kind of announcement this morning." Alex released her and turned to get up. "I hope he has more information by now."

Once ready, they proceeded down the hallway several steps until Alex stopped in front of their room.

"I wonder if I could..." He tried the door knob, but it was locked.

"Your medicine?" she asked.

"Yeah. I've got to take it. If I don't, I could be inviting a seizure to occur. You know." He looked around as if for advice.

"Let's go ask if Doug will okay us going in there," she suggested. Missy knew firsthand the gravity of his concern.

He took her hand and they began to descend the stairs together.

When they reached the first floor, they heard footsteps approaching hurriedly.

"Alex, Missy, I was just coming to talk to you."

"Sam, I need to get my medication. Is it all right to use my room key?"

The paramedic nodded, and the Marcuses turned to retrace their steps. Sam looked at Alex silently and jerked his head toward Missy.

While unlocking the room door, Alex said to his wife, "Missy, why don't you go down and get a table for us at breakfast?"

"Alex!"

"Go ahead. We'll be right down."

She turned to go obediently.

Once inside the room, Sam closed the door and switched on the light. Everything was as it had been before, seemingly normal, except for the opened bottle of pills still lying on the bathroom counter. There was also the chalked outline on the floor where Burt had lain.

Pointing, Sam said, "Those are your pills, Alex." Then, after a slight pause, he added, "The police tested a couple to be sure of the content. Believe it or not, all of them are still there, somehow, as far as I know. They were counted. No evidence was found here, so you can take the bottle."

"And Burt?"

"The police think it was an accidental fall." Sam sighed and then continued. "He must have gone into your room by mistake, thinking it was his, gone to the bathroom to get a pill for his headache, lost his balance, fallen, and hit his head hard enough to kill him."

When he had finished gathering up his medication, Alex replaced the cap and put the bottle in his shirt pocket. Coming out of the bathroom, he heard Sam's question.

"Aren't you going to take one?"

"I always take it with a meal, so that I don't forget it. Usually, when I go back for seconds, even if it's just something to drink, I'll go into the restroom and take it. Then I go get my seconds, whatever it is."

Sam chuckled softly. "And I thought you were just a big eater."

Alex's expression grew more serious. "Sam, do you really think it's that simple?"

The other man shrugged.

"So the police aren't going to investigate further?"

"Not unless they're given another reason to, I guess," Sam replied.

"Can someone hit his head hard enough to kill himself?" Alex persisted.

"It's possible, especially if you sever a pressure point." Sam put a hand on Alex's shoulder. "Come on, Dick Tracy, let's go get some breakfast so you can take your medicine."

They walked to the door in silence. As they were leaving, Alex asked Sam if he and Missy could go back to their original room that evening.

"I don't know," Sam replied. "You'll have to ask Doug."

Following the morning exercise session Doug made a similar announcement, although less detailed. He added that Ray would be attending the funeral to represent the ski lodge.

Brenda received the news with open sobs. Everyone else remained in shocked silence until Marie voiced the simple irony.

"Just like that, he hit his head and died."

"A sudden death is always hard to accept," her father said slowly.

Clara, unable to hold in her frustrations any longer, blurted out, "See, I told you it was predicted. Remember?"

All eyes turned toward her.

"What do you mean predicted?" Doug asked.

"The Card of Death. I drew the Card of Death during my—"

"She doesn't know what she's saying," Gloria Johnson

interrupted her.

Doug scowled at his wife. "I think she does," he muttered.

Doug held up his hands for attention, and those who could see began to shush the others, quietly quelling the stirring murmurs.

"I think the best thing we can do for Burt is to continue as usual. He loved a good time, and he wouldn't want to spoil the party, I'm sure. A brisk run will clear our heads. Gloria, come with me." He led her to their room for a private discussion while the instructors took over with their students.

Lessons began, and Missy threw herself into the effort.

"Come on back and start over., Sandy shouted. When Missy had reached her side, Sandy asked her what was wrong.

"I didn't sleep well last night. I just couldn't. I had this stupid dream about...well, never mind."

"No, go on, tell me," Sandy encouraged. "Maybe you'll feel better afterward."

Missy looked at her instructor and said, "I dreamed that Clara was arrested for Burt's murder."

"Ooh. No one said anything about murder," Sandy responded. "Do you think it was?"

Missy shook her head quickly. "I told you it was a dumb dream."

Sandy nodded. "Ready to go again?"

Missy nodded and took her position. This time, she was able to hold her balance as well as her thoughts in check.

"Okay, Alex, go forward," Sandy urged him.

He too traversed the slope in good form.

"Clara, stop!" Sam shouted as he skied after her. She had been using her poles to pick up speed. He shouted directions to her to keep her on the trail. She had crossed the open slope and had continued, unknowingly, away from the open area and onto a trail that wound into the woods among the trees. Sam repeated, "Clara, stop!"

When an obstruction bumped the top of her head, Clara tumbled in unexpected surprise.

Sam came quickly to examine her. "Are you hurt?"

She shook her head slowly. "No, I guess not. What did you do? Throw a rock at me?"

"Of course not." Surprise added pitch to his voice. "I told you to stop, Clara. You were headed out of bounds onto the woods trail outside of our open area. A tree branch brushed the top of your head."

She sighed. "Oh, all right. I'm sorry. I just wish that I could get away...from myself, you know? I wish I could be someone else, or something."

"Tell me what's wrong." Gently Sam took her hand in both of his. "Let me help you, Clara."

She shook her head, and her breathing became labored. "I—I don't know, Sam. I mean, even Dr. Sorenson hasn't been able to stop the nightmares."

"Let it out. Talk to me," Sam implored while still holding onto her hand.

"I—I—Toms say that I mustn't tell anyone."

"Tom? Why?"

She began to shake with sobs as her body tried to defend against the threat of invasion into the privacy of her twisted mind. "Because then you'll know...that I—I'm *crazy*!" She almost screamed the last word hysterically.

Sam released the hand to put his arms around her, trying to comfort and reassure her as well as prevent her from running away. "Clara, listen to me. You are not crazy. You're normal, like the rest of us. Do you understand me?"

Like an obedient child, she allowed him to embrace her

without resistance. "You don't know," she protested weakly while still shaking.

"Then trust me, Clara. You can tell me. Don't be afraid. I already know that you're taking sleeping medication for your nightmares." Sam ventured into the truth. "I know that you're a subject in dream therapy."

She stiffened under his touch.

"I just don't know the reason for the dreams." He fell silent, allowing her time to absorb this information.

One hand reached up to smooth the silky, black hair that covered her head. Her hood had fallen back to expose its beauty. He realized that his own heartbeat had accelerated. He knew the warm feeling within was due to her closeness.

"Please, let me share your burden. It can't be as terrible as you think. It's the loneliness that's scary."

"When I was in high school," she began, "there was a fire in the gymnasium. The fire was set deliberately." She took in a deep breath, then let it out slowly and shakily. "It was set by another student, named Arthur Wills. He set it because he was trying to kill me. They said he was crazy. He had asked me out, but I wouldn't go out with him. He set it for revenge. I'm not so beautiful, Sam. I have scars. Dr. Sorenson is trying to help me forget, but I can't stop the dreams. Sometimes the dreams are so wild...and I cannot tell the difference between them and when it's real. You see? I *am* crazy, too!"

"No, Clara. No you are not." Sam pulled her into a tight embrace, trying to shield her, comfort her, and protect her from the memories.

She clung to him as deep sobs expressed the pain inside her.

Sam allowed her time to cry. While holding her patiently, he was praying silently for her.

Finally she calmed and slipped her arms out from behind him.

He touched both of her cheeks with warm fingertips. Then his lips were covering hers. Sensing her tension, he withdrew after a moment.

"Please, Sam. I'm confused enough."

"I'm sorry, Clara. I know I promised to wait until you asked. Oh, Clara, you are beautiful. I want you to trust me and feel free to confide in me. I do care for you, Clara."

"Sam." She tried to make it sound like a protest and shook her head for emphasis.

"It's all right. I can wait for you. Just say you'll let me be your friend, okay? I'll be here for you if you need me. I promise, Clara."

"Thank you, Sam. I'm glad for that."

She heard the swish of nylon as he stood. Then she felt the warmth of his still ungloved hands as he helped her to her feet

"We'd better get back before they form a search party," Sam said.

When they reached the clearing, the distant echo hailed them.

"We're coming!" Sam shouted in response. "Clara, go straight ahead. Can you follow the voices?" Then he shouted again. "Keep calling, Alex!"

Clara listened, then started to push herself forward up the incline using her poles and walking her skis. Sam followed. When they had almost reached the other party that was gathering, Sam spoke to Clara again. "Very good tracking, Clara. That was a successful exercise."

Realizing that he was trying to avoid explanations on her behalf, Clara thanked him enthusiastically. Then she smiled for the others.

"Sam, you could have let one of us know before you set out to test Clara's auditory skills," Sandy protested. "You know the rules."

He nodded briefly. "Sorry. It was a sudden impulse."

"There won't be a next time, will there, Sam?" Doug said rather than asked.

"No, sir," Sam replied obediently.

Doug continued, "No unnecessary chances need to be taken. There should be no more accidents. I've already spoken to Gloria, and as for you, Clara, practicing on your own is your business. But what goes on while you're here is ours. Am I clear?" Doug waited.

Clara nodded silently.

"Good. Now it's almost lunchtime, so let's all go back inside." Doug led the procession of skiers while Ray brought up the rear.

While at lunch Clara muttered to her fork of green beans, "No one can tell you what to believe."

"What did she say?" Missy asked.

Alex repeated for his wife and then added his agreement.

"My belief is my choice," Clara said louder, more assured of her conviction.

"Sometimes, though," Sam said, "people make wrong choices."

Clara raised her head as if to look at him. Sam sat across the table from her. "Who is to say what is wrong?" she asked.

"When the facts are...mixed up or misunderstood, then wrong choices can result," Alex said.

"How can one know if the facts are mixed up?"

"That depends on the individual circumstances," Alex replied, and then he picked up his tea cup.

Clara picked up her piece of bread and asked him to

explain.

Alex replaced his cup on its saucer and sat for a moment to think over his words. Finally, he began, "Well, it's a matter of trust. How reliable is the source of information you're using?"

Sam made a noise and nodded his approval.

"What do you mean?" Clara asked again.

"If you're using, say, an encyclopedia or world atlas to look up facts," Missy said quickly, "you can be pretty sure that you're getting the proper information. These books have to meet standards of authority and accuracy in order to be published as reliable sources."

"Thanks, honey." Alex sounded pleased. Then he continued. "It's a little harder if your source is a person, for example. Then you must evaluate the credibility of that individual."

"That's where trust becomes extremely important," Sam supplied emphatically. "Is this person interested genuinely in your welfare?"

Clara nodded while swallowing, then agreed. "Yes, yes, I see."

The chair groaned as Alex pushed it back. "Excuse me for a few minutes. Now, Missy, don't tell me. You want another piece of pie?" He was smiling.

This time his wife shook her head. "No, actually I'd like another fruit salad. It was tasty. Oh, and my tea, of course."

"Me, too," Clara added. "For the fruit salad and the pie."

"Okay. Anyone else?" Alex asked.

"Yeah," Sam decided. "I'll have the pie and coffee and fruit salad."

Alex chuckled a little as he left the table.

"He's so good to me." Missy smiled wistfully. She was still smiling when he returned.

"Ah, thank you, my friend," Sam responded when Alex set

the tray down and distributed the assortment of items he had brought back.

Alex continued to set Missy's items on her tray and verbally explain positioning to Clara as he assisted her. Her pie was at six o'clock and the salad at two o'clock, as if there were an imaginary clock lying face up on the table in front of her. She understood the clock method of reference for placement of her items.

"Oh, thank you, Alex, but I forgot to ask for another drink."

"I'll get it for you, Clara," Sam offered.

"I believe I will choose coffee this time. Thank you, Sam."

Sam was gone only briefly. The others ate in silence during his absence.

"I keep expecting to hear Burt yelling about something," Missy said hesitantly. "It almost seems quiet without him."

"Yes. That was too bad that he had that accident," Clara said.

"We don't even know if he was a Christian, although it didn't appear so," Alex reminded.

"What difference is that?" Clara asked. "He believed whatever he wanted to. Right?"

Sam explained. "It's just that those of us who are Christians believe that we are assured of eternal life after death through Salvation and the redemption of Jesus Christ for those who believe in Him."

"There are many theories about the afterlife," Clara said.

"Christians don't believe in reincarnation," Missy explained, "because, according to the book of Hebrews 9:27, 'It is appointed to man once to die and then the judgment;...'" She raised the spoon to her mouth.

"I suppose you don't interpret the stars, either?" her friend asked.

"Well, that isn't exactly true, but the inf—"

"Missy," Alex interrupted her, "what do you mean?"

"I've read a book that explains the Gospel according to the constellations. It says that the twelve signs of the Zodiac are actually different pictures of Christ's story. But the correct interpretation of these has become misconstrued, and the study of astrology has been twisted," Missy said.

"I don't believe you," Clara said simply. "I'm going up to my room for a while to listen to my music before we begin again." She stood. "Excuse me."

"Clara." Sam stood also.

"I know my way, Sam. See you in a little while." Her cane tapped and banged as she moved among the tables and chairs to leave the room.

Sam sat back down to finish his meal.

Missy looked toward her husband. "I hope I didn't offend her."

"It's not your fault Missy," Sam said quickly. "You know how Satan likes to deceive the mind, and hers is too easily influenced. I made some real progress with her this morning. That wasn't a test run out there. She had run off scared and gotten herself off track and into the woods. Of course I followed, and I caught up with her when she fell. She started to open up to me a little. Apparently Tom has her convinced that she's crazy. But more than that, her dreams are scaring her—dreams about her past."

"Sam, we know more about her past than you would think."

"How's that, Alex?"

"Go ahead, tell him," Missy urged.

Alex reached over to squeeze her hand and then withdrew his. He began to briefly explain to Sam. "Clara and Missy were both victims of a twisted mind. The same man who had set the high–school fire that was intended to kill Clara tried it again, only my wife was the next target."

Missy said, "Arthur Wills, haunted by his own recollection of his past, mistook me for Clara and tried to rid himself of the nagging truth by trying to kill me."

"How could someone mistake you for Clara? You don't even look alike."

This time, Alex answered. "It didn't matter, Sam. Art thought Missy was Clara. That was enough. At first, he used false bomb threats, then pranks, and a couple of attempts failed. Finally, he knocked her unconscious, tied her up, and started a fire in her room. It was spring weekend. Most everyone had left campus, except for a handful of students. I had gone home myself but decided to come back early. Thank God I found her in time."

"The names sound kind of similar," Missy added. "Well, maybe in a general way: Clarissa Méndez, Melissa Sanders." She shrugged. "Actually, I got a Valentines card for Clarissa Sanders."

"Unbelievable," Sam said after a pause. "I had no idea."

"Now you'll understand when I say that Tom Hawkins reminds me of Art Wills," Missy added. "He gives me the creeps."

"Really?" Sam responded.

"Missy, I told you not to let your imagination run wild."

"Wait a minute, Alex," Sam said. "You know, Clara recently told me that Tom has convinced her not to share her feelings with anyone because the other person might think she was crazy."

"It's not crazy to have nightmares." Missy swallowed the remains of her now cold tea.

"Of course not," Sam agreed.

"So the speech about trust was for Clara's benefit? Figures," Alex said. "How did you get her to open up to you, Sam?"

"I just happened to be the one who was there at the time she broke down," Sam said. "She was ready to run off by herself, to try to get away from her own past. She fears her own dreams." Sam sighed.

"Dreams can be very scary." Missy spoke emphatically.

"Yes, but not being able to distinguish the difference between nightmares and reality is even scarier," Alex pointed out in a serious tone.

Sam nodded. "I think she does realize that. She just doesn't know how to cope. God, I wish I could help her."

"Let's pray," Missy suggested.

The three of them joined hands to do so.

Soon afterward, Sam knocked a second time on Clara's door.

"Who's there?" Clara called from inside.

"It's Sam. It is time for lessons."

"I'll be down in a minute."

He heard the music stop as Clara clicked the tape recorder off. Sam waited until she came out into the hallway and closed her door. "Clara."

Startled by the unexpected voice, Clara jumped slightly. "Sam, I told you I'd be right down. I do know my way."

"I know you do, Clara. I just wanted to wait for you. Is that all right?"

"No." The cane began to tap as Clara moved forward.

Sam followed dejectedly. As they neared the landing for the stairs, he heard her mumble.

"Trust Tom."

When they were all outside, ready to begin, Sam asked her, "Maybe you'd rather have Tom guide you for this lesson, Clara?"

"Yes," she replied.

Sam gestured, and Tom came forward to instruct her while

Sam oversaw them both.

What's wrong with me, now? Sam wondered. He was confused by her abrupt change of attitude.

"Keep talking to her, Tom. She needs to know where you are as a point of reference."

"Okay. Keep going straight. That's good, Clara," Tom complied.

Following the afternoon session, Alex and Missy were almost to the top of the stairs when Gloria Johnson appeared at the foot. She told Alex that he had a phone call. Missy continued on to their room while he went to answer it.

Missy had been making entries in her notebook regarding their trip. A writer can use all sorts of information for articles or stories, so she kept a running file for future reference. Again she looked at her watch, which seemed to make the time pass even more slowly. Alex had been gone a long time.

Finally she exchanged her notebook for her Bible, deciding to reread some scripture verses about patience. She was paging through the book of Proverbs when her husband opened the room door. Before she had a chance to ask, he spoke.

"Come on, Missy. It's time to go eat supper."

She closed her Bible, replaced it on the night stand, and got up to go with him. While he was locking the door, she asked the question.

"After Pete's call, I met Sam, who was in the hallway waiting for me. He wanted to talk about Clara. I'll tell you all about things later. Have you seen Clara since we were at lunch?"

She shook her head.

"Sam said she was acting very strangely this afternoon," Alex told his wife.

"Alex, do you see Clara?" Missy asked him when they had joined the line in the dining room.

After searching for a moment, Alex replied, "Yeah, she's sitting with Tom and Marie."

"Shall we join them?"

Alex, followed by Missy, approached the table in question. "May we sit down and join you?" he asked politely.

"Sure thing," Tom responded congenially. "Food's good tonight. Isn't it, Clara?"

"Yes."

"This trip is more fun than I thought it would be," Marie said.

"How's that?" Missy asked.

"I was afraid that there wouldn't be anyone my age, and there isn't, but it doesn't matter. I'm having a great time, anyway."

"That's great, Marie," Missy said. Then she asked casually, "How about you, Clara?"

"Yes. I've already told you that I love to ski," Clara answered. "It makes me feel free." Then she felt around the food on her plate with her fork.

"Hello everyone."

Faces turned toward the voice.

"Sam, have a seat," Alex offered quickly.

"I have the night off, and Doug gives us free time," Sam explained.

"Free time," Clara repeated. "I wish I could ski and ski until I drop."

"I can take you out if you want to go," Sam offered.

Tom raised his coffee cup to his lips, but Alex saw the corners of his mouth stretch into a subdued grin.

"Good," Clara said as she stabbed at her food.

"Don't hurry," Sam told her. "We'll want to wait until the meal digests. Besides, I just got here to get my supper, anyway."

Tom stood. "Excuse me while I go get some more coffee."

Missy leaned over to survey her husband's plate, which was almost empty. She looked up and asked quietly, "Alex, aren't you going back for something else, yourself?"

"Hmm. I don't know."

She stared at him for a moment.

"What's the matter?" he asked her. "Do you want something else?"

"Alex, you usually go back for a reason."

"Oh, you mean—Yeah, of course. It just slipped my mind, I guess."

"Alex, are you all right?" She was genuinely concerned.

"Yeah, sure. I'm fine. What did you want?"

Missy sighed and then chose tea and dessert without really thinking about either.

As if reading her thoughts, Sam spoke with resolved assurance. "Everyone forgets once in a while, Missy. Surely you've forgotten something important or misplaced something that you use all the time?"

She nodded.

"I sure have," Marie agreed.

Tom returned then with a basket of biscuits, which he placed in the middle of the table, announcing their presence, before he sat down with his coffee. Once seated, he took a biscuit, buttered it, and passed it to Clara. Then he told her, "Biscuit at six o'clock, Clara." He dropped it onto her plate.

"Thank you, Tom," she replied automatically.

"Are you feeling okay, Clara?" Marie asked her roommate.

"Yes. I just want to get back outside. It's so fresh out of doors."

"Can't argue with that," Alex stated as he reached for a biscuit himself.

"It's too bad about Burt," Marie said suddenly. "I mean, it's weird that someone could fall, hit his head, and die so easy."

"Accidental death is harder to accept because there is no time to prepare for it psychologically beforehand," Alex explained. "It's too unexpected, and the mind has to adjust."

"Yeah, well, I'm finished. Excuse me," Marie said and stood to pick up her tray.

"Are you going to our room?" Clara asked.

"Just for a minute," Marie answered. "I'll be with my parents for a while. I finally convinced them to play Monopoly with me. I knew I brought it for a reason. See ya later."

"Have fun, Marie," Missy said.

Thinking back, Alex grinned. "My brother Ben and I played many a board game in past years. He used to try to cheat and then accuse me of doing it. We had plenty of arguments, too. Then we spent more time looking for lost pieces than actually playing. Sometimes, it took until the next day to find them all."

"The games were short in my family," Sam explained, "with so many younger ones around. It seemed that I was always teaching it to one of my brothers or sisters or one of their friends."

"Never played it," Clara said simply.

"It's a board game dealing with buying and selling property," Missy explained. "There's a braille version, and the game is computerized now."

"Yes, I've heard," her friend replied. "It doesn't interest me."

"She just likes to ski," Sam asserted. Then, turning toward Alex he asked, "Do you and Missy want to join us?"

"Well, I'm not sure. Missy?"

"No, I don't think so," his wife responded. "We'll find something to do." She replaced her tea cup and pushed back her chair.

Without a word, Alex stood also. The jubilant expression that he wore needed no speeches.

Sam was chuckling softly. "See you tomorrow."

Clara seemed oblivious to the turn of the discussion. She sighed and put down her fork. "I'm finished, Sam. I'd like to go back to my room for a while, all right? You may come for me when you're ready."

"Clara, are you feeling all right?"

She nodded and stood. She took her tray and stepped slowly to avoid any obstacles. As if knowing that Sam would follow her, Clara continued to speak conversationally.

"I just want to relax and listen to my music tapes for a while."

They walked up stairs in silence. Sam promised himself that he would find the truth no matter what the cost.

11
Déjà Vu

"So, tell me what Pete said." Missy's voice was eager.

"Oh, yeah." Alex stretched his long legs out toward the foot of the bed and folded his arms across his chest. "Basically, he learned that there is nothing to find out." He turned his head to watch her reaction.

"Alex, be serious. How can that be?" She too folded her arms across her stomach.

"Dr. Sorenson is a brilliant researcher in dream psychology, and the list of his degrees and honors is staggering. When Pete interviewed him—"

"Pete actually talked to the mystery man?" she interrupted.

Alex nodded. "When Pete talked to him, the doctor pulled the Fifth Amendment, and that was that."

She thought momentarily, then said, "You mean he had no comment?"

"Precisely, Mrs. Watson."

"He wouldn't even say anything about Clara?"

"Nope. That's Pete's exact quote." Alex uncrossed his arms.

"Now what do we do?" his bride asked him.

Warm hands invited her into pleasing enclosure.

"Nothing we can do. Pete's the best. If he can't get anywhere, how do you expect us to?"

"Alex?"

"Missy, I'm tired. Just rest with me a while."

She made a sound of contentment, wrapped in his arms, while her mind raced, searching for a verse about God's perfect rest. She thanked Him sincerely for her new husband. They snuggled together. Soon they drifted into sleep.

Time eludes the sleeper, carrying him away from the cares and concerns of the present. It gathers him up like a snowball and rolls him deeper into uncertainty and the unexpected.

After a time, the knocking at their door shook Alex awake from the avalanche of his fitful dreams.

"Coming," he called. "Just a minute."

His wife sat up when she heard his voice. "What?" she asked.

Alex strode barefoot to the door and ran a hand through his ruffled hair. "Who is it?"

He was tucking his shirt back into place. He glanced around to see that his wife had also risen to comb her hair and straighten her clothes, and she was putting on her hearing aids.

"It's Sam. May I come in for a few minutes?"

Alex opened the door and greeted his friend with a smile.

"I'm sorry," Sam apologized. "I just needed to talk."

"No problem," Missy said. "Would you two like me to leave the room?" She was still standing.

Sam shook his head. "No, of course not. Actually, Missy, I'd welcome your input, also."

"Clara, right?" Alex sat back on the edge of the bed and gestured for Sam to take a chair.

"I just can't figure her out," Sam confessed. He pulled out

the desk chair and brought it closer to sit down. "One minute, she's cold as ice, and then when you break the surface, she's warm and wonderful. Then she freezes again. I just can't seem to get through to her. I mean, the person she really is under that—that snow job she pulls."

"She's had her own problems, Sam. Maybe she needs more time," Missy suggested.

Sam shook his head. "No, it's more than that. I almost got her to open up a little to me this morning. She started to tell me about her past, the fire, her nightmares. But tonight, she was back to the old facade again. Didn't either of you notice at supper tonight?"

"I really wasn't paying much attention," Alex admitted. "My mind was wandering a little, too. The automatic tone of hers seems normal to me, I guess. For her, I mean."

"But that's just it," Sam pointed out. "It's that automatic tone."

"What are you getting at, Sam?" Missy asked.

"It sounds unnatural, automatic, uh, well, trance like."

"Like hypnosis?" Alex suggested.

Sam nodded. "I was afraid to say it, you know, like I was crazy. But that's exactly what Clara thinks about herself."

"Wait a minute, Sam. Clara thinks she's crazy?"

"Well, not exactly, Missy. Tom has her convinced that if she confides in anyone, that person will think so."

"Tom?" Alex asked. "Why?"

Sam shrugged.

"Maybe he's trying to protect her defenses."

"Oh, come on, Alex."

"Hear me out, Missy. If Clara isn't ready to face her fears, Tom could be using the fear of disbelief to shield her until she's ready to face the truth."

Missy made a grunting sound. "Alex, could Clara really be hypnotized?"

"I'd say it's unlikely. Certainly not all the time. Who would do such a thing, anyway, and for what reason?"

"Tom," Missy said flatly.

"What motive?" her husband asked.

"I don't know," Missy snapped back.

"You know," Sam remembered, "Clara told me once that she was afraid of Tom. Then, later on, she was mumbling something about trusting him."

Alex nudged his wife's side. "Women do change their minds."

"Yes, and so do men." She folded her arms emphatically.

"You know," Alex suggested, "it doesn't have to be by hypnosis for one person to have control over another. There are other means."

"Yeah, like blackmail, threat, abuse, greed," Missy said. Then she added as an afterthought, "How about astrology?"

"Good point," her husband agreed.

"Yeah, I've tried to dissuade her from it myself, but she's as loyal to that as...I am to...to Jesus," Sam said slowly. Following a silence, Sam spoke again. "I know what power is controlling her now."

Alex also formulated the inference. "But, Sam, who is he using as his leverage?"

Missy wiggled a bit to change her position. "Greater is He who is in us—" she began to quote.

"Yes, than he who is in the world," Sam finished. "But if we agree that there's some kind of external control in the physical sense, then who is it, and why?"

"And how?" Missy asked.

"Astrology is a better guess than hypnosis," Alex suggested.

"Many people are dedicated to following it."

Sam silently nodded his agreement.

"I read a book about astrology once," Missy offered. "It explained how each sign of the Zodiac is really a picture of God's plan of salvation, but it has been twisted and distorted through the years into something else. You know, the way the meaning of Easter and Christmas has been distorted and commercialized by the worldly view." She sighed. "I wish now that I could remember the details of the account."

"Missy, do you mean to say that you think Gloria Johnson is behind Clara's strange behavior?" Sam shook his head. "That seems hard to believe. Besides, Clara hasn't been here very long."

Alex agreed with Sam. "It doesn't seem too likely that it would be her, although it could be. Maybe someone in Clara's recent past has significant influence over her thinking."

"Right. And how do we find that out?" Missy asked. "Well, I know one thing. We have got to fight with prayer to get Clara over to our side."

The two men nodded and exchanged grim looks.

Sam stood. "I am going to the kitchen for some coffee and a snack. It's only a quarter till midnight, but it's about the time I come back from my other job, when I'm working. Join me?"

"After we pray," Missy agreed. She bounced across the bed so that the three of them could join hands as heads bowed.

The following day, Ray and Brenda were absent from the group to attend Burt's funeral in his home town. The others gathered as usual for lessons.

Sandy watched complacently as Missy tromped back up the incline after the last run of the morning session. As her pupil approached, Sandy made the decision to ask. Waiting until Missy was close enough to hear her, Sandy voiced her opinion. "You're doing fine, Missy. Everything was executed correctly, but I have the feeling that you really weren't here today. Didn't you sleep well last night?"

"Ah, to sleep. Perchance to dream. I'm sorry. I've been working on a theory of sorts. I really didn't realize that I was that preoccupied."

Alex approached then, breathing deeply. "Getting better?" It was almost a sigh.

Sandy nodded her approval. "You'll be turning pro before we know it."

Alex waved away the jest. "I've been observing Clara," he said. "She seems to be a different person on the slope. No wonder she enjoys skiing so much."

"Different how?" his wife asked.

"More confident, I guess. She seems to know what she's doing and where she's going."

"Why? Don't we?"

Alex shook his head. "Now, I didn't say that. I wasn't talking about us at all, Missy."

She put her hands on her hips, allowing her ski poles to dangle from the wrist bands. "Well, aren't we looking smart, too?"

"Very smart," Sandy affirmed. "Come on. It's time for lunch."

"Let's go, fair lady." Alex bent down to remove his ski tip from a clump of snow. When he straightened, he saw her smile. At the grumbling of his stomach, he resisted the temptation to hug her. He smiled back. It didn't matter if she could see it or not. His special endearment had not lost its charm.

"What?" Alex's attention was finally on the speaker who

had repeated his name a couple of times now.

"You came in looking pleased with yourself," Sam observed. "Have a good run this morning?"

Alex grinned and nodded. "Nice to be in control once in a while."

"Please elaborate," Sam urged him.

Alex replaced the skis and poles in their places and turned to walk a few paces with his friend.

"Haven't you ever just said the right thing to make a woman's face light up, and you felt like you were up in the clouds? You know, one of those rare occasions?"

Sam was nodding. "Well then, congratulations. But, beware. They say the honeymoon won't last."

"Who says?" Missy interjected. She had approached and was close enough to hear Sam's last comment.

"Just kidding," Sam replied quickly.

Laughing silently, Alex put a hand on his friend's shoulder. "Sam, this sure isn't one of those times for you."

Sam agreed with a chuckle. "Not lately."

Missy stepped closer to her spouse. "Alex, I have an idea."

"Uh oh." Alex placed his arm around her shoulders as they walked. "I have an idea, too, but I can't express it here."

"Oh, be serious," she chided. "I wonder if Doug will allow me to use the library." She turned her head. "Sam?"

"I don't know. You can ask him." Sam glanced around. "Where's Clara?"

Once inside the dining room, Alex spotted Clara and Tom already seated.

"I thought she was still putting her gear away, and then I lost track of her while I was talking to you two. She's a real mystery, Alex."

Alex turned to face his friend. "One I am sure you would

love to solve," he teased.

Sam nodded soberly.

"We'll help any way we can," Alex assured him.

"Thanks both of you," Sam replied.

The knock on the door startled Alex to wakefulness. Then he heard a voice call in low tones, "Time out, you two. Show's on."

Still a little disoriented, Alex strode over to the door to open it. "Missy's not here," he told Tom, who was smirking at him on the other side.

"Oh? Want me to go find her for you? Everyone else is eating by now."

"No, that's all right. I know where she is. I didn't realize the time. We'll be in shortly."

Tom nodded briefly and left Alex alone to recover. He had not been aware that he had fallen asleep.

Didn't think I was that tired, he thought. Missy must still be in the library.

After closing and locking the door, he went into the bathroom to refresh himself.

Supper time already? Upon catching a glimpse of his reflection in the mirror, he stared momentarily. He then switched on the light, but it did nothing to help the pallor of his skin.

Hearing a rattle, he knew that his wife had returned and was unlocking the door.

"Alex?"

"I'm in the bathroom." He picked up a comb and passed it through his golden waves to straighten them.

"Hey, I couldn't wait to get back to show you what I've found," she chattered gleefully as she approached him. "You'll never—Alex—"

His arms were squeezing her tightly, and then his breath tickled her ear through her hearing aid as he spoke softly into it. "Missed you, love."

"Mm." She returned his affection. Then she asked, "Is something wrong? Usually you're reminding me when it's time to eat, and it must be past that now, I bet."

He drew his arms from behind her back. "Yeah, it is. Tom came to get us, but you hadn't gotten back yet. I didn't tell him where you were."

She nodded. "Ready?"

She reached for his hand as they walked. She continued to chatter as they descended the stairs to the first floor. "Anyway, I found a copy of the very book I was talking about, *The Gospel in the Stars* by Joseph A. Seiss. I couldn't believe it. Is God with us, or what? Then I found a lot on astrology, of course, but get this, there was something on subliminal suggestion and hypnosis. I can't wait to get back upstairs and start reading. Alex, are you listening?"

"Yes, darling. I know how you feel about books. But let's not discuss it around the others. Okay?"

She nodded her agreement.

When they entered the dining room, there was no line to hinder their approach.

"Well, you almost missed it this time," Gloria said to them.

"Sorry. We lost track of time," Alex apologized.

"Hmph." She responded with a grunting sound.

"Is it still okay to have seconds?" Alex asked her.

She nodded.

"What did she say?" Missy asked as they walked to find a table.

"Yes," he replied. He led her to sit with Marie and her

parents.

"Going to the party tonight?" Marie asked them, after greetings had been exchanged. "I am."

"I don't think so this time," Missy answered.

"Good for you," Marie's mother approved. "Newlyweds should have some time to spend alone together."

"Exactly," Alex agreed with her, but not for the reason that she had implied.

Missy's closed–mouth smile added credence to the facade as she continued to chew her food.

Marie's father observed casually that he had seen Clara and Tom together a lot recently.

"Yeah, I've hardly seen Clara at all today, except for skiing," Marie said. "I wish there were more people here my age."

Once they had returned to their room, Missy went straight to her desk and sat down.

A little while later she heard a chair being dragged and looked up to see her husband, now wearing pajamas, seating himself beside her.

"Bedtime already?" she asked.

"No, just being comfortable. Now, then, Mrs. Watson, let's see what you've got."

"Alex, do you think Gloria did it?"

"Did what?"

"Killed Burt."

"The police ruled it an accident."

She put down her magnifying glass to squirm sideways in her chair and look up at him.

"I know, but you don't buy that any more than I do. Come on, tell me what you really think."

He answered seriously. "I think it's too soon to make any outright assumptions. Stop and think about it. We don't know who had a motive, really. Besides, who is to say if there's any connection between that incident and Clara's strange behavior?"

"Do you think there is?"

He shook his head. "I don't know yet."

She nodded and turned back to her books.

Alex took one also and began to explore its pages.

Several hours had passed when Alex heard the faint sound of hurrying feet.

"Missy, something's happening."

He stood and went to the bed to grab his robe. Then he went to the door of their room.

As he opened the door, he witnessed Clara frantically waving her cane and tapping it in a random, unpatterned clamor. He stepped out into the hall and spoke as he approached her.

"Clara, it's Alex. May I help you find your way?"

"Alex! Please let me come into your room. I—I—need to talk to somebody. Please!"

He allowed her to take his arm to guide her steps. He announced to Missy that Clara needed to talk and led her to the chair by his desk.

"I was with Gloria." She began to cry. "It happened again. Gloria said that—" Clara wiped her eyes with a hand. Her speech was erratic. "—the cards do not lie. I'm sorry."

"Try to calm down, Clara," Missy urged.

Clara nodded, and her breath came shakily. "Again...I drew the Card of Death!" She was sobbing openly now.

Alex straightened and folded his arms across his chest.

"Déjà vu," Missy said.

12
Confrontations

It took almost an hour to calm Clara to the point of facing the prospect of sleep. When Missy returned from seeing her safely to her room, Alex was already in bed himself. The corners of her mouth turned upward while her heart leaped. She was still feeling the elation of a new bride. Silently she offered up a prayer of thanksgiving to God for his goodness to her. She knew her love for Alex could withstand any test. She wished that other people could have the same confidence and security she felt in her spouse's feelings.

Once she had changed, Missy switched off the bedside lamp that Alex had left on for her and slipped beneath the covers, hoping not to disturb her noble knight.

The following morning Alex maneuvered himself and Missy behind Clara and Marie in the breakfast line. "Good morning, ladies," he greeted them pleasantly. Then he asked quickly, "Clara, may we sit with you at breakfast this morning?"

"Yes," she replied, without turning her head toward the voice.

"Clara, did you sleep well?" Missy asked.

Clara shrugged in response.

"How are you today, Marie?" Missy asked next.

"Just great," the young woman replied. "This is the best school vacation ever."

Missy giggled slightly, then answered her. "I have to say this is the best honeymoon ever! I'll never forget this trip."

Alex was smiling broadly.

"Morning everyone," Sam called as he approached to stand behind Alex in the line.

The others chorused back their greeting in unison.

Sam stepped sideways to reach out and touch Clara's arm. "May I sit with you this morning, pretty lady?"

"Yes."

His warm, pleasant demeanor had no impact on her monotone response. She had answered Alex in the same manner previously.

Sam persisted. "Clara, are you all right?"

This time, she took in a deep breath and then responded, "I'm fine." She exhaled with a sigh.

"You can move up a couple of steps now, Clara," her roommate told her. "The line is moving a little bit."

Sam stepped back into the line, and Missy slipped her arm around her husband's waist. Finally they moved through the line to get their food and be seated. Once at their table, Sam tried again to converse with the object of his attention.

"I heard you were upset last night. I'm sorry. But I'm sure you will feel better after the morning run, huh? Clara?"

"You heard?" she repeated. "Hmm. People should mind their own business."

"You asked us for help last night, Clara," Alex reminded her.

"Maybe, but still, you should not have told Sam."

"I'm sorry, Clara," Sam apologized. "However, I'm very concerned about you and how you're feeling and that you can't change."

Clara continued to eat in silence.

While sipping her tea, Missy wondered if she should ask Clara what her horoscope for the day read. She looked up as Tom passed by their table and gestured a greeting.

"Morning, all. Hey, Clara, watch those snowballs. Now have a cheery day. Bye."

Clara waved and smiled as Tom walked away.

If she could have seen well enough, Missy would have also exchanged glances of surprise with her husband and Sam.

"What's his secret?" Sam muttered.

Alex had discerned the phrase. He asked, "How do you feel now, Clara?"

Clara raised her chin and replied, "I'm ready to go. And you, Alex?"

"Just great." There was an unnatural depth to his tone. He saw Missy glance in the general direction that Tom had taken, but before she could open her mouth to speak, he nudged her leg with his knee under the table. This was an indication to her to keep silent.

Instead, she said, "I hope there are still doughnuts left, Alex."

"All right, I'll go." He tried to sound grudging.

"That's a good idea," Marie agreed.

"I'll go with you, Alex." Sam also stood. "I could use another cup of coffee."

"Me, too, please," Clara said.

"Right," Sam replied.

"Alex."

"Don't worry, honey. I won't forget."

Missy nodded silently. She wished that she had an excuse so that she could go to hear their conversation, but she remained seated with Clara and Marie. "I wish I had thought of bringing my music tapes with me," she remarked casually to the other two.

"I brought my radio," Marie said. "I use my earphones now, like Clara does."

"Mm." Once she had finished chewing and swallowing, Missy remarked, "I don't really listen to the radio much. I'd rather read and concentrate on what I'm reading."

"Don't you get books on tape?" Marie asked.

"I did in college," Missy said. "I tend to fall asleep listening, I'm afraid."

Marie giggled. "Then you should take up knitting, or something. I do it."

"Really? That's great. Isn't it, Clara?"

Clara grunted and nodded. Then they ate in silence until the men returned.

"Mm. Thanks." Missy waited no longer to sample another pastry.

"That's all right," Alex assured her. "I told Sam to make sure Sandy works you extra hard this morning." He grinned.

She nodded while she ate.

"Doughnut, Clara?" Sam offered.

She held out her hand for the item but said nothing.

"The food's good here," Marie stated as she reached for the plate of goodies.

"Sure is," Sam agreed. "That's all the more reason to exercise and stay in shape."

"Uh oh," Missy mumbled.

"Missy, remember how we used to take long walks just to get away for a while and talk?" her husband reminded her. She was smiling radiantly, so he continued. "Well, now we'll have to invest in some skis."

She rose to give him a warm hug and then sat down again. With sudden realization, she added, "Alex, that's a wonderful idea. Let's go for a walk now, I mean, when we're finished eating. That's exercise right?"

"Okay, I'm just about ready." He finished his food and drink.

When she was ready, they rose and excused themselves then left the table.

When they were dressed and out of doors, Missy began to question.

"Alex, what did you and Sam have to talk about when you were alone? Clara's strange behavior, I'll bet. I wonder how Tom can change her mood so easily when no one else can. That's what I wanted to say earlier when you stopped me."

Her husband nodded. "Yes, darling, I know what you mean. But in itself, it proves nothing. Don't forget, Tom is her guide. Her doctor put him in charge of her welfare on this vacation trip. I would venture to say that she was under some kind of hypnosis, but it isn't that simple, to just say a word and hypnotize someone. It takes preconditioning."

"So you still think Gloria Johnson has her under some kind of spell?"

"I wouldn't put it exactly that way."

"Well, how can we find out?" his wife persisted.

"If I knew the answer to that, the rest would be easy."

He stopped walking, stooped to scoop up some snow and form a snowball. Then he tossed it up in the air and caught it again.

"Remember what Tom said to her? Watch out for snowballs?"

"Hey, wait a minute." Missy stepped back and raised her

mitted hands.

"Now, I'm not going to throw it at you, sweetheart."

"Well, then, what do you think?"

"I'm not sure, yet," her husband replied.

"Maybe Tom's planning a snowball fight."

"Why would Tom do that?"

Two startled faces turned toward the voice which belonged to the object of their speculation. Preoccupation had prevented their heeding Tom's approach. However, Tom misinterpreted their motivation because of the newness of their marriage.

"Not a bad idea upon second thought, however," Tom saod pleasantly. "I seem to find you two alone a lot off in the corner, so to speak, huh?"

Missy felt the hot blush of guilt, as if she had just been caught stealing cookies from his jar.

"Morning session's coming up," Tom reminded them. "Are you two coming back to join the group, or are you planning to go off alone?"

"Of course not," Alex retorted. "You're making—"

"Avalanches out of snowballs?" Tom suggested wryly.

"Not funny," Missy mumbled. "Alex?" Her hand was reaching out but not finding his.

Alex patted his snowball audibly and then threw it down. "I'm right here, Missy." He stepped closer and took her mittened hand in his. Her grip communicated her desire to remain in close contact with him.

During the morning announcements, Doug assigned the regroupings in which the instructors would now become spectators. Their sighted trainees would now pair up to instruct the less visual members of the group to ski on. The regular instructors would only intervene if necessary. Alex and Missy would be paired together, Tom and Clara, Marie and one parent, and so on. Notice was taken that Brenda remained paired with Ray. Doug explained it as being due to the fact that she had arrived by herself and she had requested to remain with her professional instructor.

Once outside, Sandy motioned to Alex and Missy. "Follow me. We're going to branch out," she told them.

They followed her away from the lodge, down a slight incline, to an area of trees where a series of paths twined around.

"Since Missy has some sight, we'll use a more complicated terrain," Sandy explained.

She gestured and indicated for Alex to choose a trail where he would lead his wife through the course and back around to where Sandy would wait for them. Once she had described to him the conditions of the area he had chosen, they were ready to begin.

Time passed quickly as their confidence grew with practice. They were descending for the fourth time when, in the middle of a cleared area, Sandy heard Alex shout, "Stop! Stop!"

As Sandy approached from a short distance away, she saw Missy obey quickly. Missy turned halfway around to see her husband slump to the ground. She began to walk clumsily on skis back up to help him.

"Alex, what is it?" Sandy asked bewildered.

"Alex, can you hear me?" Missy asked in a matter-of-fact tone of voice.

"Yes. Yes," ge replied. "I just felt suddenly weak and dizzy."

"Sandy, is he pale? Are his eyes glazed?" Missy asked.

"His eyes are clear and focused, but he is a little pale," the instructor answered her. "What is it Missy?"

"I'm all right, honey," Alex said. "I remember everything. I just felt dizzy for a few minutes."

"Maybe you should go back to the lodge and rest for a while," Sandy suggested.

Alex nodded. "Yeah, I'll do that," he agreed. "You two continue your lesson."

"But, Alex, I don't want to leave you," Missy protested.

"I am all right, honey." He got to his feet and balanced on his skis. "Don't worry. It isn't what you think. I'll tell Sam first chance I get. I promise. Go ahead with Sandy now and enjoy your lesson. You'll be coming in soon, anyway." He turned to go back.

"You think it's more than just dizziness, Missy?" Sandy asked her once Alex had gone.

Missy sighed and shrugged. "I guess not."

She didn't want to explain her husband's epileptic condition. After all, she thought, he would also be disoriented if a seizure had occurred. He seemed to be steady on his feet when he left. Dizziness in itself was an oddity, though.

Following the session, when Missy had finished stowing her equipment, she turned to find her husband waiting for her. Eagerly she entered his open arms to return his brisk hug.

A deep voice beside them interrupted their union. "Hey, you two, acting like newlyweds again."

Missy sighed while Alex greeted the speaker.

"I hear you took a dive this morning Alex," Tom continued.

Alex nodded and released his bride.

"Are you okay?" Tom asked him.

"Fine," Alex replied. "Thanks."

"It happens to the best of us," Tom said. Then he called, "Clara, are you ready yet?"

A moment later the lady walked toward the sound of his voice with accurate steps. "Yes, Tom."

The two of them moved away toward the dining room.

"Since when is Tom so concerned about you?" Missy asked.

A hand came to rest on Alex's shoulder. "How are you?" Sam asked him, and then he added, "Boy, I can't even get to first base. I feel like I'm a third party."

"Don't give up, Sam," Alex advised. "Clara doesn't even know her own mind."

"Isn't that the truth," Missy agreed.

"Let's go eat," Alex suggested. "I'm hungry."

They began to walk together.

"Mind if I sit with you two?" Sam asked.

"Our pleasure," Missy replied and gave him a genuine smile.

Once they were standing in line, she asked, "How does Tom keep on top of everything? He seems to know about everything that happens."

"Especially when it concerns Clara," Sam added.

When they started toward the table area, they came within hearing range of an argument in progress between the Johnsons.

"—how I feel about it." Doug's voice began to rise in pitch.

"Yes, but you can't control the spirits. Nor can I," Gloria countered.

"What is it going to take to make you stop this nonsense?"

"She came to me, Doug. I won't refuse anyone who asks for my help in such matters."

Doug and Gloria could not be seen because they were in the back kitchen area, but they were clearly heard. There was little other noise to detract from their dispute except for an occasional clink of silverware on a plate.

"Gloria," Sam called, "there are still three of us who need to be served."

She came around quickly, apologized, and began to set up

more plates.

"Doug, may I speak with you?" Clara called.

While waiting for Doug to come around to their table, Tom studied his companion in silence.

"Yes, Clara?" Doug said when he arrived. He remained standing.

Tom gestured toward a chair, but Doug shook his head.

Clara began, "It seems to me that one should be allowed to exercise his or her own free will as long as it does not interfere with other people." Clara spoke boldly. "If I choose to consult someone who is knowledgeable in what I seek, I see nothing wrong in that. Your wife is a gifted psychic who could help those who believe in this ability. I don't think that you have the right to prevent her from using her gift for the benefit of others."

"That stuff is nonsense," Doug replied. "So I guess you're telling me that you intend to continue with her as long as you're staying here. Is that it?"

"Yes."

"Well, go ahead, then. Play your silly games. Nonsense, if you ask me. Nothing but rubbish." He began to walk away. "I'll have nothing to do with it, that's for sure."

Tom reached across the table to touch Clara's hand briefly. "Clara, you surprise me."

"I believe in the power of the stars," she said simply. "There is no law against practicing what you believe."

"I couldn't agree more," Tom replied. "It's all a matter of perspective and control."

"What is she saying?" Missy asked.

"Clara said that she believes in the power of the stars," Alex repeated for his wife.

"How about the power of the Gospel?" she countered.

"Then Tom said it was all a matter of perspective and

control," Sam added.

"Control," Missy echoed. "You mean, like a controlled experiment?"

"Now, that's an interesting thought," Alex observed.

"How so, Alex?" Sam asked.

"Oh, nothing, really. I was just thinking like a psychologist, I guess. You know, as in a controlled group in behavior analysis."

Sam nodded and they fell silent to continue their meal.

When they were nearly finished, Missy commented, "I've never seen Clara so assertive." Then she turned to her husband to ask him, "Alex, are you skiing this afternoon?"

"Mm," he answered while chewing.

"I may not agree with Gloria's psychic power," Sam commented, "but her cooking is great."

"Yes I'll agree to that." Alex rose from his chair. "I'm going to get some more meat. Missy?"

"Please, some more tea, another fruit salad, and some more dessert, okay?"

Her husband chuckled. "My sweet loves sweets, Sam."

"Yeah, I'll second that order, except coffee instead of tea, Alex, if you don't mind."

"Right, Sam."

"At least we can say that we're working it off," Missy commented. "No wonder you don't see many overweight skiing instructors."

This brought a chuckle from Sam. "You and Alex make quite a team. How did you meet?"

She replied, "We met in college. He was worship leader for the Christian fellowship group that I belonged to. It was a small college, but I didn't really get to know him until my sophomore year. He was a junior then."

Sam sighed. "I'd certainly like to get to know Clara better.

She's here for such a short time. I just don't seem to be able to make any progress with her."

Missy nodded. "She'd make a good study subject for Alex, with her strange behavior."

When Alex returned and distributed the items, they began to eat in silence again. Sam looked up when he saw Tom and Clara approaching their table.

"Clara says she's willing to work with you, Sam, so I'll leave her with you for a while." Without another word, Tom turned to leave the room.

"Will you sit with us?" Sam asked as he stood and gently guided her to a chair next to his. "It's always a pleasure to have your company. May I get you anything?"

"No, thank you."

"Clara, it's Missy. I've been meaning to ask you if I might borrow one of your music tapes again. I wish I'd thought to bring some of mine."

"All right. Which one do you want?"

"Do you have any on marriage?"

Clara shook her head and then replied no. "Oh, but there is one on love. Perhaps that one?"

"Yes, all right. Thank you. Oh, by the way, that was quite an interesting speech you gave Doug this morning."

Alex and Sam exchanged unseen glances of surprise and misgiving.

"It was the truth," Clara stated.

"Isn't truth a matter of interpretation, too?" Alex asked.

"That depends on the basis of it. The cards don't lie. You can't dispute their truth. It exists and it can be proven."

Missy was not up for an existential debate, but she was prepared to defend the Gospel. Aloud, she said, "Proven how?"

"That's for the psychics to determine. I don't know how."

Braving it, Missy began her argument based on her research. "Clara, what if I could show you another interpretation of this truth based on the stars?"

"Yes?"

"Tonight," Alex suggested, seizing the opportunity. "Why don't we get together tonight for a B—" He almost bit his tongue, not wanting to dissuade her curiosity by mentioning Bible study. Correcting himself, he amended, "Basic study in our room. Say, about eight o'clock?"

Clara was nodding, and Alex told his wife so.

"Am I invited?" Sam asked quickly.

"Naturally," Alex replied.

"When you're ready, Missy, I'll go and get you the tape."

The others took their cues from Clara and stood, preparing to leave the table.

Once outside, Sam directed Clara's descent into the skiing lesson.

When they had traveled some distance and made several runs, they stopped to rest, sitting against a tree near the trail.

Clara said happily, "I feel great today. I love being out here in the open air."

"I'm very glad you're enjoying this Clara. I'm also enjoying being alone with you."

"Sam, don't talk like that."

"Why not? It's true."

"There's much you don't know about me."

She turned her face away, but his gloved hand caught it under her chin and brought it back toward him.

"Then tell me, Clara. Tell me the truth."

"Sam, don't bring up the past, please. Not now. Don't spoil a beautiful day. There are not many happy ones."

"Why not, Clara? It doesn't have to be this way. Can't you

see? I want to change that for you. Clara, trust me."

"I don't trust myself," she retorted with inflection to her tone. "Sometimes I feel like my life is someone else's and not my own, as if I do things that I wouldn't do, and then the nightmares...I thought I had gotten rid of the dreams about the fire when I was in high school. I was severely burned...and scarred. Then the dreams came back again, and others, too. Why do you keep bringing this up to me?" The tears burned in her eyes, but she continued. "When I ski, I feel like I'm free. I'm myself, and this is my will and my freedom to really be me. Then you come along and spoil it by reminding me, always reminding me of the bad things."

"Clara...Clara..." His arms reached to enfold her, but she pulled back to avoid him.

She scrambled to her feet. "I want to ski, Sam. I want to ski until I drop."

He also stood and resumed the role of guide instructor.

Oh, Clara, he thought, there are many things that you don't see.

Lord, he prayed, help me to keep trying to reach her for her own sanity and her soul.

13
The Power of the Gospel

"Alex, this is a wonderful honeymoon," Missy confessed when they had returned to their room that afternoon. "It was wonderful having you guide me."

He took this as an invitation for a thank-you and came to collect his kisses.

"Alex, it's time to study," she said softly.

"Hmm." He bent his head again.

"No, no, the books. I want to be ready for Clara tonight."

"No, my love," he retorted in a whisper. Then he lifted his head to answer her. "No excuses, now. We're not dating. We're married. You aren't teaching school. This is our vacation, after all. Darling, you can teach me about you...."

With a joyful sound, she tightened her hug while he lifted her off her feet to carry her to the bed.

When he had laid her down, there came a knock on their door. He immediately put his hand over her mouth to keep her from responding. Seconds later, the knock repeated, and Sam called Alex's name. With a sigh, he went to answer the door.

"May I come in for a couple of minutes?" Sam asked.

"Sure," Alex replied.

Missy had risen and was seated at her desk. "Hi, Sam. Did you have fun with Clara this afternoon?"

"No, that's just it." Sam sat on the edge of the bed while Alex pulled out the other desk chair for himself. Sam continued, "I tried to get her to face her fears, but it backfired. I guess I had better not come here tonight for the Bible study. She might leave if I show up. What a way to ruin a night off!"

"Let us talk to her for a while, and come by later," Alex suggested. "Wait about twenty or thirty minutes, and then knock."

"I don't know if I should. I don't want to drive her any further away. Do you really think I should chance it?"

His friend nodded. "All she can do is leave the room."

"Yeah, I suppose so," Sam agreed. "Well, I'll get going and let you two study. Thanks. I'll see you at supper."

While Alex went to close the door, Missy got up to put Clara's tape into her tape recorder. "It's almost supper time already," she said.

When she turned around, her spouse stood close.

He began gently to move her backward and down onto the bed.

"I love you." He sighed the words close to her ear and began again to kiss her warmly while the tape played.

When they finally arrived down stairs for the evening meal, they were the end to a nonexistent line in getting their meals.

"The newlyweds are late again," Tom observed in a voice that was loud enough for all to hear.

"Get a girlfriend," Missy mumbled, but Alex heard and chuckled.

"Hi, Sam," Alex greeted heartily as they sat.

"Hi, Alex, Missy," Sam responded.

"Sounds like you could use some cheering up," Missy commented. "Why don't you borrow this *Love* tape of Clara's? We were playing it before we came down."

"It's that good you had to finish listening to it before you came down to supper?" he asked innocently.

"Something like that," Alex stated.

Sam shrugged. "Why not? But let's not mention it to Clara, okay? I've done enough to upset her already."

Alex nodded his agreement and picked up his cup of tea.

"Keep the faith," Missy said simply.

Sam nodded.

They continued to eat silently.

After a time, Alex announced that he was going to go back for seconds and asked if anyone else wanted more to eat.

"What are you getting?" his wife asked.

"Hot chocolate," he replied in a flat tone.

"What did you say?" she asked.

"Hot chocolate," he repeated in the same tone.

"Alex, that isn't what you usually have," Missy commented.

He repeated the same phrase, turned, and walked away from the table.

"Maybe he just wanted a change," Sam suggested.

Missy shook her head. "But it's the repetitive phrase and the way he said it."

"Yes, I know what you're thinking, Missy," Sam commented. "But one incident doesn't mean anything, in itself."

"Yeah, I know." She finished chewing her mouthful then mused, "I wonder if he'll come back with hot chocolate or tea."

After a pause, Sam said, "You know, if you take Clara's behavior by itself, one incident, it doesn't seem so strange. But when you put it all together…I just don't know what to think."

"Mm. Sam, why don't I go and get that music tape for you

now, while I'm thinking of it? If Alex comes back, tell him I would like some more tea and another fruit cup. I did say tea."

"Will do."

When Alex returned, Sam explained to him where his wife had gone.

Alex had brought her some tea and dessert. Upon placing his items and taking his seat, Alex commented to Sam, "Gloria made a mistake. She gave me hot chocolate instead of tea. I can't imagine why. I know I asked for tea for myself."

"Tell you what," Sam offered, "I'll take the chocolate and go get you some tea. I need to get up, anyway. I'll bring a fruit cup for Missy, too."

"Thanks, Sam." Alex began to eat his own meal.

Missy returned to the table just ahead of Sam. Once she was seated, she asked her husband what he was drinking.

"Tea, of course." he replied casually. Then he explained the mistake of receiving the wrong beverage when he went to get it.

"Well, you said it three times before you left the table," she pointed out to him.

"What?"

"You repeated hot chocolate three times when you got up."

Alex shook his head. "I couldn't have. I don't remember."

"You did," Sam agreed. "I heard you, too. Don't worry about it, Alex. There's enough strange behavior around here to let something else bother us."

"Where is Clara, anyway?" Missy asked tactlessly.

"She's sitting with Tom and Marie," Sam answered. Then he asked, "Are you ready to convert Clara's astrological mindset?"

Missy sighed.

"Well, I wouldn't put it quite that way, but let's hope so," Alex said.

Sam nodded. "I don't know if I should come by or not."

"How about if you wait a little while, then come in," Alex proposed.

"Yes, good idea. In the meantime, I can be praying."

"That's another great idea," Missy said.

"No activities scheduled tonight? Isn't that unusual?" Sam asked them. "I know I'm working most of the time, but I thought that there was always something going on in the evening."

"Nothing formal, as far as we know," Missy said. "But I think you can always use the reception room."

"Yes, that's true," Sam said.

"Missy, are you finished yet?" her husband asked.

"Almost done." She began to eat faster.

It was not quite five minutes before the hour when Clara knocked at the Marcus's door. Alex greeted her and guided her to a chair beside the desk where his wife sat.

"Thank you for coming, Clara."

Clara nodded slightly.

Alex's voice came from in front of her. "We really didn't know anything about astrology until we started studying for tonight, Clara. Missy borrowed some books from the library downstairs, with Doug's permission, of course."

"So you're able to read print all right, Missy?"

"Yes, Clara. I have a special magnifying glass that makes the print seem larger."

"She uses tapes too," Alex offered.

"So do I," Clara agreed. "But of course, I also read braille."

"I don't have the feeling in my fingers for it," Missy said. "I've known some braille readers to be faster than sighted people, though. I teach special education classes at a public high school back home."

Clara turned her face toward the sound of her friend's voice. "I went to public high school, too. It was in Troy, New

York." Alex noticed the change and slight loss of color to her features just before she added, "That seems like such a long time ago, now."

Feeling the need to steer away from an unpleasant subject, Alex asked quickly, "How did you become interested in astrology, Clara?"

"It was at a country fair that my parents took me to. I met a soothsayer at the fair, one who foretells the future, and her prediction came true." She wiggled slightly on the seat and dropped her head momentarily. Then, after drawing in a deep breath, she continued. "A little more than a year later, the prediction came true...almost. But, please, don't ask me to explain this further. I can't. I won't do this."

Missy felt the tensing of muscles as she touched her friend's arm. "No, Clara. We won't ask you anything that you don't wish to tell us. We just want to learn from you and show you our way of thinking. That's all, honestly."

Clara sighed and pulled her arm free. "Yes? All right, then."

"We're from New Hampshire, Clara," Alex tried again to lighten the conversation. Then he asked her, "Have you ever skied before coming here? This is my first time. In fact, Missy had to coax me into this trip."

"Really?" Her head rose again. "I've never skied before, but I'm determined to find a way to continue. I love it now that I'm here."

"What made you decide to come here, then?"

"Dr. Sorenson—Ah, I mean, my, uh, physician rec—I mean, he told me about this place, and he suggested it would be a good place to have a rest—a restful...vacation."

Alex agreed simply.

Searching for some safe area of conversation, Missy said,, "It was nice of Tom to come with you so that you wouldn't have to travel alone."

"Oh, yes, Tom."

Alex noticed that her body tensed even more. Finally, he suggested, "Clara, if we're making you feel uncomfortable, we can continue this another time."

The darker head shook in protest. "I'm sorry. It's me, not the two of you. I've had some problems, that is all."

"We'd like to help if we can," Alex offered again. "Now, that's all I am going to say about that. Tell us how you feel about God, Clara."

"God? Well, I never really thought about it that way. you see, everything has a cause–and–effect relationship. The alignment of the heavenly bodies, the planets, stars, and moon, directly affects events and behavior here on earth. I've had events foretold, and not always happy ones."

"But how do these things come about?" Missy asked spontaneously.

"I don't know," Clara admitted. "I don't know all about it. I only know what affects me most."

"That's g—" Missy's sentence was interrupted by a knock at their door.

"Come in," Alex called from his seat.

The sound of the voice that followed made Clara's heart beat increase noticeably to her.

"I didn't know you had company. I just wanted to…"

"Come sit down, Sam," Alex offered as the voice trailed off. Then he turned his head. "Do you mind, Clara? Sam is also a Christian. Maybe he can help explain things as well."

"Yes, it's nice to see you, Sam," Clara responded truthfully.

Alex rose to give his friend the chair, and he went to sit on the foot of the bed. "We were discussing astrology and Christianity. Now, what were you saying, Missy?"

His wife thought momentarily. "Oh, I said that it's good that you're interested in things that affect you, Clara, because God is personal, too. In fact, this is the basic foundation of a healthy spiritual relationship with Him."

"So, you believe in the spirit world also?" Clara asked.

"I don't think our interpretation is the same as yours, Clara," Alex said, feeling the need for clarification. "You see, we believe in God's Holy Spirit, or Holy Ghost, also called the Comforter, who leads us into the understanding of spiritual truth."

"Yes," his wife agreed, "and that's the first principle of the Bible. Well, I mean one of the first. It's that God must be worshiped in spirit and in truth."

"Who knows what is truth?" Clara asked.

"Now, that's a question that man has been asking since time began," Sam commented.

"Wait, I can define it." Missy reached for her Bible as books thumped on her desk. "I mean, the Bible can." She began noisily to turn pages, then started to read when she found the place she wanted. "'Whatever is true, whatever is honorable, whatever is right, whatever is pure, whatever is lovely, whatever is of good repute, if there is any excellence, and anything worthy of praise, let your mind dwell on these things.' That's from Philippians 4:8. And there's another verse. 'Be ye transformed by the renewing of your mind,' which is fr—"

"Missy," Alex interrupted, "slow down. Take it easy. We don't have to overwhelm her, you know. Excuse her, Clara. She gets a bit overenthusiastic at times."

"That's all right." A faint smile crossed her red lips. "I like that saying. Are there any more like that one?"

"Oh, yes," Missy answered quickly. "You know, you can get a braille Bible if you like, and it's also available on cassette and computer disk."

"Yes, I've heard of this," Clara answered. "But where is this God in the universe?"

"God is the Creator of all things," Sam explained. "'Before the creation of the world, He was. He made the universe and all that is in it. Nature is too perfectly precise to have just happened or evolved, and if it did just happen, why only one time?"

"And why haven't we evolved to a higher level yet?" Missy asked.

"It probably just hasn't occurred yet," Clara offered.

The short silence that followed was broken by Missy. "We forgot to mention someone," she reminded the men. "You know, Jesus, God's only begotten Son, the One who died as sacrifice for us all so that we can, by faith, accept His ransom in our place to resolve a right relationship with God the Father and Creator. There is nothing made or known that God does not foreknow."

"Clara," Alex picked up the explanation, "that's the personal part. Each one of us has a choice to individually accept or reject God's Son's free gift of Salvation and the presence of God's Holy Spirit, who will by faith lead us into His truth for us."

"And you do not lose your free will, Clara," Sam added. "In every decision, every situation, you have the right to choose the path you wish to take. You can be obedient to God or disobedient."

"I never heard it that way before," Clara admitted. "You mean you can do whatever you want to do?"

"Well, there are consequences to your actions," Alex clarified.

"And what about astrological predictions?" Clara asked.

"Remember when we mentioned God's Son, Jesus Christ?" Missy reminded her. After receiving a nod, she continued, "The signs of the Zodiac are actually a road map pointing the way to

Jesus."

Alex grinned at the triumphant look on his wife's face. He carried a secret pride in her enthusiastic heart for their Lord and Savior.

"How can that be?" Clara was asking.

Missy's expression changed as she was reminded of her studying. She mumbled something and turned to find her notes on the subject.

"I see you two have been hard at work," Sam commented during the paper shuffle. "Go ahead, Missy. I want to learn about this, too."

"Do you want to learn about the stars, Sam?" The eagerness in Clara's voice was undisguised.

"Only from a Christian point of view."

"But predictions work, Sam. They really do come true."

Alex wanted to be careful, but he had to ask, "How do you know, Clara?"

A silence followed, except for Missy's ruffling papers. Finally Clara spoke again. "The proof is right here in this lodge. Remember? I drew the card of Death, and now Burt is dead."

"Coincidence," Sam mumbled.

"Skeptic," Clara retorted.

"Okay, I've got it," Missy declared.

Alex silently praised God for her timing.

Looking up, Missy asked, "Okay, Clara, what's your sign?"

"Aries. The Ram."

"Okay, according to this," Missy shuffled papers again momentarily, then picked up one, "Aries means Lordly Lamb, head or chief, Prince of the flock, and Ram means great or lifted up." She looked up from her reading. "So, if Aries means Lordly and Ram means lifted up, Prince of the flock—"

"Then the sign represents the Lamb who was slain and

then glorified," Sam interpreted eagerly.

"In other words, Clara," Alex added, "it points to Jesus Christ, who is the Lamb of God, the Good Shepherd, and we are the flock, His sheep. That is, if we accept His free gift of Salvation, then we will share in His heavenly inheritance."

"I never heard this before," Clara admitted meekly.

Missy picked up her paper again and continued. "It says that the traits or characteristics of this sign include eagerness, competitiveness, impulsiveness, independence, courage—"

"Courage?" Clara questioned. "I don't think so."

"Oh, yes, Clara," Sam replied. "It takes courage to try something new, as you have, by coming here to learn to ski. You've encountered new surroundings and new people. I admire your courage, Clara. Honestly."

"I never thought of it in that way."

"Sam is right," Missy agreed. "What's your sign, Sam?"

"I think it's Leo. The Lion."

"Hey, that's my sign, too. I looked it up by my birth date."

Clara nodded at Missy's approach to the subject.

"All right, Missy, what's mine?"

Missy smiled at her husband and then answered, "Taurus. The Bull."

Sam chuckled. "What a collection. I can guess that Leo indicates the Lion of the Tribe of Judah, but what's the bull?"

"Missy?" Alex asked.

"The bull represents God's judgmental wrath, apparently. According to this book," she gestured, "there once existed a creature called a re'em, of the ox family, who killed man and beast on sight. God's wrath is for the wicked, the disobedient, who deny Jesus."

"When will this happen?" Clara asked.

Sam answered, "On the Great Judgment Day, when we have

all passed from this life to the Great White Throne Judgment of Christ, it will occur. Everyone who has ever been born will be held accountable for his or her actions, especially unconfessed sins."

"That sounds scary," Clara admitted.

"It doesn't have to be, for a Christian," Alex reminded her.

"That's what's so great about God, too," Missy added eagerly. "Each person born is given a chance, in his or her life, whether to accept or, well, reject God's gift of reconciliation. At least He keeps offering it until the person dies. If you, for example, have heard the offer, receive the invitation, and accept His gift of life eternal in His Son Jesus who became a living sacrifice for your sins, in order that you might be saved to life everlasting in His kingdom, then the Holy Spirit will teach and lead you into a closer walk of faith with the living Lord. If we are willing to confess and repent of all our sins, He is faithful to cleanse us of all unrighteousness," Missy paraphrased from I John 1:9. "Our God is a loving God, but he expects obedience and fellowship from us. The stars are a road map to this truth. Each person must choose for himself or herself to determine his or her own destiny. No one else can do it for you. This is what's so great about it. It's totally personal."

"Clara, God, through the Salvation offered in His Son Jesus Christ, can solve any problem you have, if you're willing to give it to Him," Alex explained. Then he added, "With God, nothing is impossible."

"What if you've done something bad?" Clara looked downcast.

"Each one of us has, Clara. That's the point," Alex answered. "There's no degree in this. All of us have sinned and fallen short of the glory of God. The only way to be reconciled is through Jesus. Believe me, Clara, when I tell you I've tried to mess up my happiness with my own stubborn will, but God is patient and loving. He's always there waiting for us to realize it and to call upon Him for all our needs."

Sam said gently, "This doesn't show weakness, if that's what you're thinking. It's a privilege granted to God's people by our loving, caring Father in Heaven. Take your tapes, for example. You must have talked to other Christians before this time?"

"Yes, a little." Then Clara sighed but said nothing more.

"Alex, look at this," Missy said.

Alex rose to come and look over her shoulder.

She moved her magnifying glass out of the way and pointed to the paragraph that she was talking about. Then she continued to explain. "Apparently, there are also lunar signs, as well as the solar Zodiac. Look at the word 'mansions.' Here it refers to clusters of stars making up the groupings." She glanced briefly toward Sam. "In the King James version of the Bible, it says 'In my Father's house are many mansions: If it were not so I would have told you. I go to prepare a place for you.'"

"Yes, I see," Sam agreed. He had come to look also. "You're saying the word 'mansions' has much broader implications than are usually spoken about, such as rooms in a large house. Then Jesus actually meant that the very stars in the heavens will be our home or dwelling place."

"And maybe there will be a group of them for each of us to call our own. I don't know," Missy speculated. "But isn't it a wonderful thought to ponder?"

"The Bible does say that we will be given new information," Alex added. "Who can know the mind of God? Right?"

Clara drew in a deep breath and then admitted, "Sometimes I am so confused. I wish—"

Her words were interrupted by a knock at the room door.

Alex rose to answer it. He held the door narrowly open. "Hello, Tom. We were studying."

"That's all right," Tom interrupted. "I was just looking for Clara."

Clara, who had stiffened at the sound of the male voice, now rose to her feet. "Here. I'm here, Tom." She spoke loudly.

"Clara, I've been looking for you." Tom entered the room to stand next to Clara and put his arm close enough to touch her hand. "I need to see you right now."

"Please excuse me," Clara said to the Marcuses.

"Yes, of course," Missy replied. "I suppose I should take these books back to the library, anyway. It was nice of Doug to let me borrow them."

Tom was walking toward the door with Clara in tow.

"Clara, may we study again sometime?" Missy called.

"Yes, thank you. Good night, Sam, Alex."

"See you later, Clara. Sleep well," Sam replied.

Once they had gone and Alex had closed the door, Sam spoke again. "He couldn't have had worse timing. It makes you wonder if he didn't plan it that way. She was beginning to soften." He stood to pace around the chair. "If only we could reach her! I'll see you two later. Thanks."

"Sam, don't forget the tape," Missy reminded him.

Sam picked up the tape from on top of the tape recorder, where he had placed it earlier, and left their room.

"Sam needs some patience," Alex commented. "Although that's hard to tell someone who's close to a situation."

His wife, who had been sorting her materials, made a noise of agreement. "Well, I'll be back in a few minutes. I have plenty of notes on the subject now." She collected a kiss, then left the room.

Soon after his wife had left, Alex was roused from his

relaxation by a loud rapping. He stretched on his way to the door.

"Do you want to go to the weight room with me, just to make sure I don't kill myself? I have to do something!"

"Sam? What have you been doing? Come in for a minute first."

Sam's expression showed impatience, but he complied. He began to explain. "I went back to my room and put Clara's tape on to listen to it. Then I got this urge to…act, strike out, do something! I can't just sit around and watch Clara destroy a beautiful life, a beautiful woman. Alex, I love her and I can't even get close enough to kiss her."

"Sam, it takes time and patience. I know you don't want to hear that right now. Come on, let's go. I'll just write Missy a note."

Upon leaving the room, Alex made sure that the door wasn't locked. He guessed that Missy hadn't taken her room key with her, since he was there when she had left. "Calm down, Sam. You're doing everything you can to help her."

Sam descended the stairs hurriedly, as if driven by an unseen spirit.

I wonder what's come over him? Alex thought as he followed at a lesser pace.

A short time later, Missy leaned against the closed door to catch her breath after she had run up the stairs to her room.

"Alex!" she called hoarsely.

When he didn't answer, she called again louder. With no response, she flicked on the overhead room light switch and began to search around. She went quickly into the bathroom but found no one.

"Kidnapped!" her mind screamed at her. As her heartbeat increased even more, she fought the irrational tears. Feeling weak in the knees, she went to sit at the desk where she had so recently presented her Gospel lesson of the stars.

Seeing a loose square of white scrap paper, she reached out to pick it up. She was about to place it inside the cover of her Bible, but the handwriting caught her attention. It looked as though Alex had written her a note. Taking her magnifying glass to read it, she learned that he had just gone to the exercise room with Sam.

The tears were now of relief. She got up and slammed the door behind her on her way out of the room. She needed her husband's solace now.

She was crying openly when she entered the exercise room.

Her husband was soon by her side, questioning and calming her.

It took several minutes for her to quiet enough to speak clearly. She had already become overtired because of the lateness of the hour, and any incident would trigger a torrent of emotions.

Sam had stopped his vigorous workout to come to her side.

While still holding her, Alex urged, "Missy, tell us what's wrong, honey."

Between sobs, she expelled the words. "There's a b–body...in the li–library. I—I think someone is dead!"

14
The Second Death

The next morning, Alex listened to the murmur of speculations that hovered above the dining room like a congregation of demons. His steps were slow, and his movements were unconsciously automatic. He didn't even look back to be sure that his wife was following him as she was in the habit of doing.

For some, the night had ended all too quickly, while for others, the morning activities had become a welcome diversion.

"Alex!" Sam repeated his call, and this time, Alex looked toward him.

Alex nodded a brief acknowledgement and turned to his wife. "Come this way, Missy."

"I'm coming," she answered. Once seated, she asked, "Where's Clara?"

"She's sitting with Tom and Brenda," Sam told her.

"Hi," Marie said. "Missy I heard you found—"

"Yes." Missy's quick response was a bit sharper than she had intended it to be.

"Marie is very curious," Sam stated.

Alex agreed.

"Well, who was it?" Marie persisted.

Missy shook her head and began to breathe faster and irregularly. "I don't even know."

"I'm sorry, Missy," Marie apologized as she suddenly realized that murder was real.

"Sit down, Marie," Sam offered. "I believe it was one of the maintenance workers."

Missy sighed and then asked him, "What actually happened?"

"He was hit from behind with a hardcover braille book," Sam explained.

"Isn't that ironic?" Missy said, as much to herself as to anyone else.

"Are all of us suspects?" Marie had to ask.

Sam shook his head then said, "I really don't know."

"Well, none of us at this table read braille," Marie insisted.

Alex coughed and then took a sip of tea. Finally he said, "Marie, there had to be a certain amount of force behind the blow to do that, even though the big hardcover books are heavy. It doesn't mean that the person who did this was a braille reader Anyone could have done it."

"The police are sure thi—that it was murder this time?"

"Yes, Missy," Sam answered.

Silence intruded while they finished eating their meal.

In his concluding statement that morning, following his brief summation of events, Doug asked for complete cooperation from his guests with the routine police investigation, as if it were necessary to ask, and he also promised that lessons would continue as usual.

"Thank God for that," Clara muttered.

Determination seemed to flourish during the skiing session that morning. Everyone seemed to be particularly concentrating on the task at hand. Tom and Clara, however, had gone off on their own adventure down a farther slope, away from the others.

"Alex, I think we've found a new hobby." Missy looked up at her spouse as they walked back into the lodge together.

He began to reply but had to clear his throat first for the words to come forth. "Maybe so."

"Are you okay, honey?"

"Yeah, just a little sore throat."

"Sore throat?" she repeated.

The sound he made warned her to change the subject.

"Anyway," she continued, "do you think we might get some skis of our own when we get home?"

"What? No snowmobile?" he asked.

She shook her head.

"I don't know. We'll see," he answered. Following a pause, he took her arm to draw her aside into the reception room. "Missy, I want you to be extra careful from now on."

"Alex? How do you mean, extra careful?"

"Well, just watch out and be alert, especially when you're alone. Okay?"

She nodded briefly and then grimaced.

Not wanting to belabor the subject, Alex suggested that they go back to rejoin the group. However, he resolved to share his suspicions with Sam at his first opportunity. Upon reentering the hallway, they were not surprised to see a man in a dark blue uniform approaching them.

"Mr. and Mrs. Marcus?"

Alex nodded and responded to the gestured greeting.

"I'd like to ask you some questions, Ms. Marcus."

"Yes, I know," Missy replied. She was still holding her husband's hand.

Her answers came responsively but routinely. She let her mind wander momentarily back to another time of questioning. It had been her first encounter with a police interrogation following an assault against her at the edge of a secluded New Hampshire college town. Then the bomb in the science lab and the arson attempt to murder her had followed. This tragic chain of events had led to her and Alex's marital reengagement.

She sighed now and murmured, "All things do work together for good for those who believe."

"What was that?" the officer asked her.

"Oh, nothing. I was just quoting a Bible verse."

The gentle pressure on her hand told her that Alex had heard it.

"Thank you for your cooperation," the officer said. "We'll be in touch, Ms. Marcus."

They continued to follow slowly behind the officer.

"It's Mrs. Marcus," Missy grumbled. "I hate Ms."

Her lover released her hand to put his arm across her shoulders. "Does this mean I can't call you 'darling' any more, Mrs. Marcus?"

She glanced up into a smiling face. With an exasperated sound she answered, "You know what I mean."

Abruptly Alex's smile faded to a more serious expression, which could be heard in his voice. "Missy, I still need to talk to Sam. He was behaving oddly last night, too."

"Sam, now? Alex, what in the world is going on around here?"

"Maybe it's not of this world." The words had slipped out spontaneously before he could stop.

His wife nodded with understanding. "Yes, and I'll bet that Gloria Johnson has something to do with it, too."

A trying day led to a restless night.

When Missy returned from the bathroom following a nightmare, she discovered her husband's absence among the flat bed covers. Switching on the bedside lamp, she was not surprised to find a note explaining that he had gone to meet with Sam when he returned from his night shift at the emergency station. She lay back down but left the lamp on for his return.

When Alex heard the click of the heavy outside door opening, he went into the hallway to greet his friend. "Hi, Sam."

Upon relocking the door, Sam turned to face his friend. "Alex, what are you doing up at midnight?"

"I couldn't sleep."

"Want to come up to my room?"

Alex nodded and followed Sam upstairs.

While removing his outer clothing, Sam gestured toward a chair.

Alex sat down then spoke. "Sam, I want to talk to you about last night. I mean, before the murder took place."

"Before? What do you mean?"

Alex started to explain, but when his voice cracked, he had to clear his throat and begin again. "Remember? You came to get me. At the time, you seemed hyped up somehow, with a lot of energy. We went to the exercise room to work it off."

Sam came to sit on the bedside facing his comrade. "Oh, yeah, that. I had almost forgotten about it. Yeah, it was kind of strange."

Alex thought momentarily, searching for an appropriate

means to convey his question without being obtrusive. "Do you have these...moods...sometimes?"

"Now, wait a minute, Alex. I'm not crazy if that's what—"

"No, Sam," Alex interrupted him quickly. " I wasn't implying that at all."

"Then what?" Sam asked.

"Odd, unusual behavior or occurrences, remember? It has happened to a number of us, Clara mainly, but also Missy, Marie, and even me, according to my worrisome wife." He paused momentarily as the frown on Sam's face faded. Then he probed, "Sam, did you do anything different that night?"

"No."

"I'm trying to find a reason or a cause for such an occurrence."

"Okay. All right. Well, let's see. I went to take a shower after coming to Bible study with you two and Clara. When I came out, I felt, sort of, like I was so excited, like I was on fire. I don't know how to describe it, but I'll never forget the feeling. It was such an intense drive to...do something. Well, you know what I mean?"

Recalling a very personal experience with his new bride, Alex said, "You mean, like an intense, overwhelming passion?"

"Ah, that's it! I just had to do something! That's when I came to get you to join me in the exercise room. "

"Sam, did you do anything else before taking that shower? Did you put the television or radio on?" Alex asked.

Sam began to shake his head and then stopped. "Wait a minute. I did play that tape of Clara's that Missy let me borrow. I hardly ever use the tape deck in my radio console, come to think of it. I put it in before I went into the bathroom, but I don't recall anything else different that night."

"Look, Sam, don't repeat this to anyone, but Missy and I had one of those intense experiences that you described."

"One?" Sam retorted.

"That isn't the point," Alex continued ignoring his dig. "I just realized now that during that time, she had one of those tapes playing, too. It happened when I came back from completing the lesson when she had the collision with Burt on the slope. I didn't think about it at the time." He waved a hand to dismiss his thoughts.

"Alex, you think there is something weird on those tapes? How could that be? They're Christian music recordings."

"Have you ever heard of subliminal messages?" Alex asked.

"Yeah, a little, I guess, but not in Christian music."

"Well, it has been done with Bible verses heard only by the subconscious mind while you're consciously listening to the lyrics. The question is, how would this have been done, and where, and when?" He folded his arms across his chest. "Sam, it has always been just Clara's tapes, right?"

Sam nodded. "You think someone has sabotaged Clara's tapes?"

"Wasn't she looking for them just after we arrived here? At the time, I just thought that she had misplaced them. I'll bet Missy remembers it."

"Then you think it was done here? But how, and more important, why?"

Alex picked up the cassette and said, "There's one way to find out what's really on here. I'll wire it to my good friend Pete Early. He's editor of the *Iandale Inkling* newspaper. I told you about him. I can trust the Early Bird to be discreet."

Sam nodded.

"Besides, if there really is a story here, then Pete will have an exclusive on it," Alex added.

"But what do we tell Clara in the meantime? She doesn't know that I borrowed it from Missy."

"Don't worry. I'll get Missy to make up something about misplacing it. She's good at misplacing things, anyway."

"Well, then, let me take it with me tomorrow. I can get it to your friend fairly quickly. It's a priority lab shipment, right?" Sam suggested.

"Great. I'll give you his address, and I'll call Pete from here."

"It'll be our secret, right?"

"Right, Sam, and you can trust Missy, also. Thanks. I'll let you get some sleep. See you tomorrow morning."

"Good night, Alex. Maybe now we'll start to get some answers."

"Yeah, instead of more questions. Good night, Sam."

Alex left and headed back to his room. "Missy, I'm glad you're still up. I want to talk to you, Mrs. Watson."

Following a warm greeting he related his story.

"It makes sense," she agreed.

"So, what will we tell Clara?" Alex asked.

After a short pause, Missy replied, "Nothing."

"We have to tell her something. She knows you have the tape."

His wife sighed and shook her head. "I know this isn't right, but I think we should let her think that I gave it back to her. She just can't find it. Alex, it was done to me! That way, it avoids complications about searching for a missing tape that, in fact, won't be here, anyway. Right?"

He pondered her proposal. Finally, he agreed.

Then she kissed him and was about to mention getting some sleep when his response changed her thinking.

The night dragged on endlessly for Alex. Yet morning came all too quickly, once his eyes had finally closed in sleep. He had to nudge his bride several times to awaken her.

When they were downstairs, Alex led his wife to the place in the breakfast line where Sam stood beside Clara. Her arm was safely tucked into Sam's, Alex noticed. Marie stood in front of them. The line seemed to move sleepily along. Alex spotted Tom's tall figure at the head of the line.

Once they were all seated, Sam began to speak to Clara, who quickly became the center of everyone's attention. "Clara, I've missed working with you. I am very glad you decided to sit with me this morning."

Clara nodded briefly.

"Let me know if there's anything in particular you want to practice. It's your choice today."

"I can't wait to get started," she said.

Missy couldn't contain her curiosity. "Clara, have you been questioned yet?" she asked. "By the police, I mean?"

Clara nodded. "Yes, and you know, I don't remember hearing anything about a murder. I must have been asleep, and that's what I said."

"Do you remember going to bed that night?" Alex probed.

Surprised looks turned his way.

Clara shook her head. "I don't remember. I must have gone to bed, of course, but I don't remember doing it."

"How about last night?" Alex continued. "Do you remember going to bed last night?"

She nodded. Then she sighed and confessed, "Sometimes I have trouble remembering events...in-—in the order that they happened. Sometimes the past and the present become confused." She shifted on her chair. "Please, could we change the subject? I'm getting a headache."

"Maybe some herbal tea would help you," Missy suggested. This thought reminded her of her friend Zoe Babette, whom she had roomed with for three years of college.

"I'll get you some, Clara," Sam offered and stood.

"All right, and another muffin, also, please?"

"Sure. Anyone else?" Sam asked.

"I'll go with you." Alex rose to his feet also.

"Alex, a doughnut and regular tea."

"Right, honey. Marie?"

"Okay, hot chocolate, but I can't decide between the two sweets."

"Don't worry," Sam replied. "We'll bring a variety. But then we'll have to work it off on the slopes. Deal?"

The others nodded their agreement.

"In spite of everything that happened, I'm still glad I came here," Clara told the other women. "I wish I could understand what's happening, though." She grew silent.

"Missy, why do you think these strange things are happening?" Marie questioned.

"I really can't say." Missy hoped that she sounded casual. "But I have faith that God knows, and He'll reveal it in time."

"Why in time?" Clara asked.

"Yeah, now would be a good time, wouldn't it?" Marie asked.

Missy took a breath and tried to explain. "God's time is not our time. The Bible says that a day to God is as a thousand years to us. We see partly, but He sees beyond our focus." Missy clasped both hands together as her joy burst forth. "There's a beautiful song about God's time. He gives us exactly what we need at the right time, not a moment before or a moment too late, but in His exact time. There are many Scriptures about time." She paused as she sorted in her mind. Then aloud she said, "Let's see, in the fullness of time, a time to every purpose under Heaven—"

"We get the idea," Marie supplied. "Right, Clara?"

Clara murmured a response.

The men returned with refreshments and seated themselves.

Seeing his wife's expression, Alex asked, "Have you been preaching again, Missy?"

"It's all right," Clara assured him. "We asked for it." Then she turned her head and asked, "Missy, do you still have one of my tapes? I can't seem to find one of them."

Missy's expression sobered as she replied, "I believe I gave it back to you." Then, after a brief pause, she added, "Don't you remember?" She held her breath, waiting for the response.

Clara merely shook her head in silence.

"I could help you look for it, Clara," Marie offered quickly. "Perhaps you just misplaced it. I do that a lot, and then I blame somebody else when I can't find what I'm looking for."

"Ah, yes," Alex agreed, "I know someone who—"

"Yes, darling," his wife finished.

"I apologize a lot," Marie added.

Upon replacing her cup, Clara stated, "I can't wait to get started. I'm ready to go skiing now, Sam."

"That's the spirit," Sam agreed.

"Glad to see you're so cheerful, Clara," Alex commented. "Actually, we're glad to see you. You haven't been around much lately."

She didn't respond.

"Clara, would you like to take a short walk with me before the morning meeting?" Sam asked.

Clare responded to this with enthusiasm and rose to leave the table. Sam had risen and was standing beside her. They left together. Alex and Missy conversed lightly with Marie until the meal was finished.

At the morning meeting before warm-up exercises, Doug

reiterated the importance of total cooperation with the police investigation, and then he thanked everyone for it.

The morning ski session progressed without incident. There seemed to be a thankfulness for routine activities to relieve the pressure of recent events.

Following the afternoon session, Alex went to talk with Gloria Johnson. He wanted to see if he could learn anything regarding her involvement, or lack of it, in the mysterious events that had recently happened.

Missy anxiously awaited his return. Finally, a tapping at their door sent her swiftly there to open it.

"What happened? Did you forget your key?" She flung the door wide open, looked up, opened her mouth to gasp, and then exclaimed, "Tom! I—I was expecting Alex. Are you looking for him?" She remained where she stood.

"Not necessarily."

The evenness in his tone made her heart beat a little faster.

"May I come in?" He pushed past her without waiting for a response.

She turned to face him but stood where she was, keeping the door open and her hand on the doorknob.

"Clara wants her tape back, Missy. I know you have it."

She shook her head. "No, honestly, I don't have it, Tom."

"Well, then, you'd better find it."

"Why does it bother you?" She swallowed with difficulty as her mouth was very dry.

"Clara is my concern." He took a step toward her. "Your husband's health should be yours. Now, if you say anything to him...Well, I was never here."

As she began to open her mouth, his hand clapped over it. Then he released her and left.

She closed the door and stood holding it shut. It was several minutes before her husband returned.

15

Confront and Confess

"What's the matter, honey? You look upset."

"Alex, Tom was just here, but he says he'll deny it if asked."

Alex folded his arms across his chest, then asked, "What did he want?"

Missy repeated the confrontation word for word, then asked about his conversation.

"Gloria was vague and evasive, as usual," her husband replied.

Missy sighed. Then she asked, "Alex, what about Clara's tape? Do you think something's wrong?"

He nodded. "Strange we haven't heard from the Early Bird yet. I can't catch him in the office or at home whenever I try." He sat on the bed.

"Maybe he's tried to call you but couldn't get through to you," his wife observed.

"You mean, you think someone doesn't want him to reach me? Someone here?"

She nodded.

"Dare I ask?"

"Gloria. Or maybe Tom. I would have included Burt, too, if he were still...here."

"Gloria and Tom have a direct connection to Clara, but Burt didn't."

"So you agree?"

"I don't know."

"Alex, what about the tape? What do we tell Clara?"

Alex didn't answer for a few moments, then he said thoughtfully, "I'll talk to Sam about it."

Sam and Clara had walked out around the inn in solitude.

"Why is life not simple?" Clara asked.

"No challenges," Sam replied, and then added, "or tests?"

"Why tests?" she asked.

"I don't know. Maybe to test our loyalty or faith or obedience. You see—"

"Sam, please, no Bible verses again. I just don't know about my faith."

"Maybe that's why, Clara, because you don't know yet how strong and courageous you really are."

She laughed a short, curt laugh. "Oh, really? How can you say? You really don't know me."

"But I want to, and I do, better than you think. Clara, if you need someone to confide in, you can trust me. I want you to know that."

She sighed. "There has been so much pain, Sam, and I still don't know why it happened to me. Sometimes I'm very confused, and I don't remember things. I have trouble separating my dreams from what's really happening. It scares me."

"Perhaps talking to someone you trust will help you to see

yourself more clearly. I could be that someone, Clara."

"But why, Sam? Do you treat all your guests this way?"

"No, Clara," he admitted. "I've tried to tell you how special you are to me."

"Please, Sam. I'm afraid."

"Then let me help you, be there for you. You don't have to face your problems alone."

The concern in his voice caused an ache in her throat. She took a deep breath to keep from crying, then in broken sentences told him of the fire in the high school gym that had left her body permanently scarred. Then she was silent.

Following a thoughtful pause, Sam explained his interpretation of beauty. "The body is just the physical. It's your soul and spirit reflected in your personality that makes someone truly beautiful. God looks at us through His perfect eyes, even though we can't see. I try to look for the good in people. There always is some if you're willing to dig deep enough to find it. I see so much tragedy, I need to keep a positive perspective to survive. Oh, Clara, I want to share my thoughts and feelings with you and want the same from you. I care so much for you."

"Sam, I can't handle this." Her voice broke into quiet sobs.

Sam pulled her into a comforting quiet embrace, and she allowed him to hold her for a time.

"You're not alone, Clara," he told her softly. "You don't have to be alone."

Sam held her quietly while offering silent prayers for her and thanking God for this beginning for himself.

Several days passed before Doug announced the results of the police investigation at the afternoon meeting. He also slated the evening social as a movie and refreshments.

"Can you believe that?" Marie queried Alex and Missy during the movie intermission. "The police ruled it an accident!"

"But you don't buy it, huh?" Alex prompted, knowing she wanted to talk about the death.

"Heck, no. I mean, come on, how could a book—especially a heavy one, like the braille dictionary—suddenly fall off the shelf just at the right moment when someone was standing there? Oh, sure it did." She shook her head and waved her hands for emphasis.

"Yes, we agree, Marie, but there seems to be no evidence to go on. No finger prints, no forced entry, no motive," Missy said.

"When they find the culprit, they'll know the motive," Marie stated.

"It would be nice if everything was that simple," Alex said. "Time to get back to our seats before the lights go out again." He ushered them forward.

Following the film, Doug stated that he had another important announcement to make. Everyone waited patiently for him to speak before getting up.

"I hate to bring you more bad news. We have certainly had enough bad tidings, this group." He paused momentarily. "Well, fact is, there's a blizzard heading our way. We may have to suspend lessons during that time. We have plenty of supplies for the duration. Usually these things are over in about a day's time, but they are a danger." Again he paused momentarily. "It's expected to be here in our area a few days from now. I'll keep you advised. Since the deaths have been ruled accidental by the local investigations, you're free to leave at any time. Thank you for your patience and continued cooperation. Good night."

"Wow!" Marie exclaimed. "This will be a vacation to remember."

"Exactly," Missy agreed.

"Alex, have you heard from your friend yet?"

Alex shook his head in reply to Sam's question. "Every time I try to reach him, I can't get through, or he's out, or something like that. It's frustrating."

"Well, I sent the package," Sam told him. "It should have arrived by now."

Alex nodded.

Sam maneuvered his way to where Clara was walking. "Clara, would you like to go for a quiet walk before bed?" he ventured and was rewarded with a quick affirmation.

After retrieving outdoor apparel, they went outside together.

"I'll never forget this time," Clara said. "In spite of all that's happened, I'm glad I came here."

"So am I, Clara," Sam said quickly. Then, after a deep breath, he asked, "Are you going to leave early, before the storm?"

"I can't."

"I don't understand."

"This isn't a vacation for me."

They walked silently for a time, hearing only the crunch of snow beneath their feet.

Finally, Clara decided to trust Sam and explained. "I'm here as a kind of therapy, not as a tourist, as everyone else thinks. I've been seeing Dr. Sorenson in New York for treatments. At first, it was just for the past, the fire I told you about. Then, while I was at his clinic, I began to suffer memory losses and sleepwalking, he told me. I'm supposed to be getting better...but...it's not working." Sobs shook her. "I'm so scared."

Sam's embrace was comforting, strong, and patient. He knew she had just taken a giant step toward her recovery, and he thanked God for it. Patiently and quietly, he allowed her time to express her pent–up emotions.

"Alex," Missy asked, "we're not going to leave early, are we?"

"No, darling. This is our honeymoon, after all."

"And it will be unforgettable! I'm still glad we came. What a surprise, actually meeting Clara."

"Let's pray for her, Missy."

"But I didn't want to leave any sooner than we absolutely had to," Marie complained the following morning.

"Your parents just don't want to take any unnecessary risks. I know you understand," Missy cajoled.

Marie nodded, but with a frown. Then she asked, "Are you and Alex leaving sooner, Missy?"

"No, Marie, but you can hardly compare a honeymoon to a vacation."

"Yeah, I know, but still I wish we could stay, too."

"I know," Missy agreed. Then she added, "You know, you can always come back another vacation. You only get one chance at a honeymoon."

"Well—"

"Hopefully," Missy added hastily.

"Well, I'm not waiting for any old blizzard. I'm outta here ASAP," Brenda declared.

"But, Brenda, haven't ya' had a good time here?" Marie asked.

"You betcha, but I see no reason to be taking risks."

"Oh," Marie said. "Clara, how about you?"

"No, I'll stay as planned. Right, Tom?"

"Absolutely."

"Skiing with me, Clara, aren't you?" Sam asked quickly.

"Yes."

"Come on, let's make the most of it," Brenda stated.

"Good advice," Alex observed.

Missy noticed a slight stuffiness in his voice.

Student and teacher grouped together and headed outside.

When the morning session had ended, Alex went to find Doug, but encountered Gloria instead. "Any calls or messages for me?"

The woman shook her head.

"I'm waiting to hear from my friend Peter Early in Iandale, New Hampshire. It's rather important."

She nodded again.

Feeling frustrated, he asked, "Any predictions about the approaching storm?"

"I don't discuss matters of the spirits with nonbelievers," she replied.

"Spirits," he repeated. "Yes, I see. You will alert me if I get any calls?"

Again she nodded.

"Well, I'll mention it to Doug, also." He turned to depart.

"No need. I'll tell him myself."

Alex left. As he walked down the corridor, he felt slightly dizzy. He leaned against the wall momentarily to rest. He covered his face with his hands waiting for the wooziness to pass.

"Hello, Alex."

Abruptly Alex dropped his hands.

"Feeling all right? You look a little flushed."

"Fine, Tom. How are you?"

"Couldn't be better. Leaving early? You never can tell about the weather, as they say."

"No, we're staying as long as we planned to. After all, it's our honeymoon."

Tom nodded shortly and walked away.

Alex stood for a few moments longer, then headed on his way to lunch. As he approached, he overheard his wife talking to Sam.

"...worried about him, Sam. You know why. It's been so long now. Nearly a year."

"Uh–uh, telling tales out of school," Alex admonished her.

She turned to see her husband standing behind her. "Oh, Alex, you know I care about you."

"She may be right, Alex. A check up wouldn't hurt, just to be sure."

"Sam, I'm all right. I'm just getting a bit of a cold," Alex assured his friend.

"Alex, why would Tom tell me to be concerned about your health?" Missy persisted.

Alex shrugged. "Who knows what Tom is thinking?"

"Or planning?" his wife asserted.

"Now, don't let your imagination run wild."

"Thank you, Sam. Finally the line is moving a little." He ushered his bride forward a few steps. Then, as an afterthought, he added, "Although, I'd be concerned about what Gloria was up to."

When the three of them had gotten their food and were seated, Missy asked where Clara was sitting.

Upon looking around, Sam saw her and reported that she and Tom were sitting by themselves at a far table.

Missy remarked that she spent a lot of time with her escort, even though at times it seemed she would prefer not to do so.

"As Gloria would say, many things are not as they seem," Alex remarked with a pronounced nasal sound in his voice.

The following day was Sam's day off from his paramedic position and the day that he received a package, the long-awaited return of Clara's tape with a message from Peter Early.

Sam went to Alex and Missy's room during the rest period following the afternoon skiing session.

"Really?" Missy exclaimed after Sam had explained and given Alex Pete's note. "I wonder who could have done that. Imagine! Subliminal messages on the tape. What's the purpose? What did it say again, Sam?"

"'Don't quench the fire,'" Sam repeated.

"What does that mean?" Missy asked. "I mean, how is it significant to anything?"

"I don't like it that Pete wasn't able to reach me," Alex said. "That shouldn't be."

Sam nodded. "Seems rather unusual to me. I've never heard of guests not getting their messages, before this."

"Now, if we could just uncover the plot and the motivation," Missy said thoughtfully. "Alex, what are subliminal messages used for, really, aside from the fiction, spy and movie stuff?"

Alex made a sniffling sound then explained, "It can be used in hypnosis to awaken an implanted response. It's called a trigger mechanism in relation to a previous directed stimulus."

"So, who besides you could know how to use hypnosis and whom to use it on? Doesn't the recipient have to be conditioned for it?" Missy asked.

"It really depends on the individual's susceptibility. Everyone is different, and we each have different tolerance thresholds."

"Well, sounds like Gloria is our prime suspect," Missy stated.

"Hey, I listened to that tape. I remember," Sam said. "It was very...stimulating." He looked at his friend. "Alex, didn't you tell me you and Missy had a similar experience while listening to it?"

Alex nodded, remembering. Then he leaned close to his wife's ear, being careful not to speak too closely to her hearing aid, and reminded her of the tape playing when he had come into their room the afternoon of her accident with Burt.

Then she recalled and nodded.

"Why Clara's tape?" Missy then asked.

"Maybe Clara's tapes," Sam corrected. "How do we tell her?"

"Okay, then, why Clara's tapes?" Missy persisted.

Alex sighed and went to sit on the bed. "You know, we were all affected by that message, and we weren't even under hypnosis."

"That's scary," his wife said. "But why Clara's tapes?"

"An easy opportunity?" Sam speculated. "She had music tapes, and someone used them."

"Used them for what purpose?" Alex asked. "To see if subliminal suggestion worked? To test a theory?"

"How about a plan, a plan for power?" Missy said thoughtfully. "Power is the ultimate goal of evil, power and control."

"I was trying to explain that to Clara," Sam said. "The difference between God's free will gift and our self-will control."

"So who is self-willed enough to want to use hypnosis to manipulate and control...what, other people...for power?" Missy asked again.

Sam shifted his position in his seat. "If we knew the answer to that, we would have our motive and some pieces to our puzzle."

"Okay, who has the technical knowhow to manipulate tapes and perform hypnosis?" Missy asked.

"Probably several of us," Sam speculated. "Myself, Alex, Doug, and maybe some more of the guests. Possibly Tom. He's a medical lab technician. Gloria might, as well. I don't know. Maybe Ray could."

Missy held up her hand. "I guess we have plenty of suspects. Now we must find out the who and how and why."

"And that's all there is to it," Sam mocked. "How do we tell Clara about her tapes? She is so confused already."

"First we need to get it back in her room. Remember, I told her I gave it back," Missy reminded them.

"Oh, I'll just put it back with the others while she and Marie are busy elsewhere," Sam offered.

"Maybe we shouldn't mention it to Clara just yet," Alex said. "She has enough problems, it seems, to deal with for now."

The other two agreed.

Sam replaced the tape while the guests were standing in the supper line that evening.

"Mission accomplished," he reported to the Marcuses as they were filling their trays with food choices.

Missy breathed a sigh of relief. She didn't like not telling the truth to anyone. Silently she wondered how she could confront Gloria and get her to confess.

16
Blizzard

Strange the operation of fate, Melissa thought.

By the following day she, Alex, Clara, and Tom were the only remaining guests. Most of the staff, the guides, had thus been given extra days off until the scheduled arrival of the next group. Sam remained because he was one of the few staff besides Doug and Gloria who also lived on the premises. Sandy had expressed a desire to help out, and Doug had offered her a room, if necessary, with the impending storm threat.

Tom had gone out of his way to remain Clara's almost constant companion, in Sam's estimation, since the majority of the guests had departed. He had not been aware of Alex's reclusiveness, as Missy had. He knew that Doug and Gloria would be double-checking and securing the lodge against the chilling conditions outside as the temperature dropped.

Somehow, though, the chill had managed to seep inside into the general atmosphere.

It began that evening. Subtly, quietly at first, the flurries went unnoticed until the howling wind urged them to speed the spread of their blanketing cover.

The evening meal had been brief, with so few people to feed. No social activities had been planned. Alex sat in front of the television while Missy and Sandy were playing cards.

"Missy, it's your turn," Sandy repeated.

Missy peered over her hand. "Oh, I'm sorry." She glanced over her shoulder at her husband before taking her turn.

"Okay, let's see." As Sandy laid down a card, the lights flickered off, then back on again.

Missy sighed. "We've had storms at home, but I can hear the wind whistling in here. That's unusual for me. Oh, my turn again?"

"Ever seen an avalanche? That's the danger around a mountain."

"Only on TV," Missy said. Abruptly she asked, "Know anything about hypnosis?"

Sandy looked up in surprise, then answered, "Not really. Why do you ask?"

Missy shrugged. "Just wondered. It gets pretty quiet around here between guests, huh?"

"Yeah, I guess. You can't be too careful with this kind of weather to contend with. We see a lot of storms and tragedies because people don't respect the danger of winter storms."

Missy nodded. Her thoughts were elsewhere. She turned her head again toward Alex.

"He looks relaxed," Sandy commented.

"Is it my turn again? I'm sorry, Sandy. I'm having trouble concentrating."

"Hard to be cooped up inside when you love the great outdoors," Sandy said, trying to project a light tone.

"Something like that," Missy replied. "Clara would probably agree."

Sandy nodded and then made an audible response. "Well,

that's it. I won."

"Oh, good." Missy's relief was plainly evident. "I think I'll see if Alex wants to go upstairs now. Maybe he's tired."

She got up and went to sit next to her husband. After several attempts, she got his attention. "Want to go upstairs now?" she asked.

Without a word, he stretched and then rose to accompany her.

On their way out of the room, she turned to Sandy. "Do you think Sam will be back tonight from the hospital?"

"I don't know. It wouldn't surprise me if he stays there overnight. He does sometimes. They may need him, anyway. He knows the danger of trying to travel in these blizzards."

"Yeah. Well, good night, Sandy."

"The storm may be over by morning, or it could stick around. We don't know yet. Have a good sleep, Missy, Alex."

"Good night," Alex said.

Once settled in bed, Missy asked, "Alex, did you take your medicine tonight?"

"Mm."

"I love you," she whispered.

In response, he snuggled closer, resting his head in her bosom, like a kitten seeking warmth and reassurance from its mother. He murmured a contented sound.

Missy brushed the hair back from his forehead. As she stroked it, her fingers felt the hot skin and cold sweat that lingered there. She touched her lips gently to his forehead. A silent prayer said she intended to seek Sam's advice at her earliest opportunity.

17
Avalanche of Fear

The following morning, Missy awoke first. She went to the window right away to survey the whitened landscape outside. Wind was throwing snow around like it was flour. Alex was still sleeping.

She was on her way out of her room after showering and dressing, hoping to find Sam, when she saw Clara approaching from her own room. Missy greeted her friend.

"Missy, I need you and Alex to come with me right away. It is important," Clara said in a monotone.

"Oh, Alex is still sleeping. Can I help you?"

Clara repeated her statement.

Tom came down the hall from the stairs at that point. "Something wrong?" he asked.

"I don't know," Missy replied. "Clara asked me to come with her. Alex is still asleep."

"Well, I guess you'd better wake him, then," Tom said.

"Why?" Missy asked.

"Because I said to." Tom pulled out a gun and pointed it close to Missy's face. "Understand?"

Silently, Missy turned to go back into her room. Now she knew it was Tom who had been hypnotizing Clara. But why?

She kept looking back over her shoulder as Tom stood in the open doorway. She went to the bed to lean over her husband. It took several attempts to coax him to wakefulness.

"Alex, here's your robe," she said, handing it to him. "We have to go."

He rose and let her help him into the bathrobe. She took his arm, and they walked together out into the hall. He seemed not to notice Tom and Clara following behind them as they walked downstairs to the living room area.

Tom directed them to be seated.

"Clara," Missy attempted to gain her friend's attention.

But Clara only stared blankly ahead.

"She won't respond to you," Tom advised. "Only to me."

He remained standing behind Clara's chair. His gun was pointed toward Missy and Alex.

Missy glanced at her husband, who was slumped in the corner of the couch next to her. His head leaned back against the upholstery, and his eyes were closed.

As if reading her thoughts, Tom said, "Sam's at the hospital, so don't expect any help from him today. As for Doug, Gloria, and Sandy, well, they're out on search and rescue. I convinced them that there was someone out skiing who got buried in a snow drift. It'll take them hours to discover nothing. Gloria is so easily influenced."

Missy tried to swallow her fear and looked in Tom's direction. "What are you going to do with us?"

"Me, nothing. It will be all Clara's doing."

"Please, Tom, let me get some medical help for Alex. You see he has—"

"Forget it. He won't be needing medical help soon. Or you,

either. Clara, I want you to—"

The sound of a door rattling and opening interrupted his command.

Missy's heart pounded harder as silence engulfed them momentarily.

Tom went to the entrance, waiting like a cat ready to pounce upon its prey. The gun rose and leveled in order to be clearly visible to the approaching figure.

"Sam, do come and join us. I insist."

The gun remained poised.

Sam, who was half out of his parka, looked up and then moved more slowly to finish taking off his coat.

Startled bewilderment increased to a new level of horror when Sam obediently preceded Tom into the room and found the Marcuses and Clara still seated there.

Sam addressed Clara and then spoke in Spanish, but neither drew a response.

"Tom's got her hypnotized, and I'm afraid for Alex," Missy said quickly.

"Over there where I can see you," Tom instructed the new arrival.

"Why?" Sam managed to blurt out as he obeyed.

"Power," Missy said simply.

"Shut up!" Tom barked. "You'll be the first to go. I swear it."

Sam prayed for a chance to rush Tom and get the gun away from him without the innocent being injured.

His gaze went toward Alex. Sam knew that his physical condition was deteriorating. The flushed features and listlessness indicated a severe cold or flulike condition. Sam, as well as Missy, knew that rundown health could be a factor for complications under any conditions. The added stress of the immediate situation only made it worse. He shared Missy's concern but tried not to show it.

Sam tried to draw Tom's attention. "So, Clara's strange behavior, you were controlling her, Tom?"

There was no answer.

Sam tried again. "Then she, under your influence, committed those murders? For what reason?"

"Think of it as a controlled experiment," Tom said evenly.

"Why Burt Franklin?" Missy asked.

Tom's gaze remained on Sam while he answered her. "Burt happened to be in the wrong place at the wrong time. He probably went into the wrong room. He was drunk, as usual, and didn't really know what he was doing. He was always getting his room number mixed up, anyway, even when he was sober. Unfortunately for him, he stumbled into something he shouldn't have. I had to stop him."

"And the other people who were murdered?" Sam asked. "Did you kill them, too?"

"No. The experiment had to be tested," Tom stated.

Missy gasped. "You mean Clara did it?" Then she ventured to ask, "What about the items that were missing...or misplaced? Remember? Several times, it was Clara's tapes, but also Marie's ski pole."

"Ha!" Tom gave a short, curt laugh. "It was easy for me to misplace things and return them later, when everyone else was downstairs, no problem."

Sam said to Missy, "Don't worry, Missy, Clara has no knowledge of anything she may have been forced to do under hypnosis. None of this can be charged against her under this condition."

Missy said softly to Sam, "I'm really worried about Alex."

"Yes, Missy, I understand."

Then Sam began to ask another pertinent question. "But

what about Alex's fi—?"

Tom cut him off. "Enough talk." Tom's voice became angry with impatience.

Tom knew nothing of Alex's condition, Sam thought, but what had he done to so influence Clara? Had he administered drugs as well as using hypnosis to gain control over her? Why Clara? Or was she just a guinea pig in a larger plan? Was she the control subject in an elaborate experiment? If so, Tom could not have engineered it alone. There must be an accomplice or mastermind. Then Sam realized: Clara's physician, Dr. Sorenson. Was he the actual schemer?

Sam was about to query Tom again, but when Sam turned his head, he saw Tom placing a second gun in Clara's grasp.

"Clara. Stand up," Tom ordered. "Trust Tom."

"What are you doing?" Missy asked.

Tom glared at her but didn't answer. Instead, he directed Clara to point the gun at Missy. Tom's gun quickly aimed at Sam, who had started to rise from his assigned seat.

Sam slumped back to a sitting position.

"Now, Clara. Pull th—"

18
The Honeymoon's Over

Tom's directions were abruptly interrupted by a loud, shrill shriek from Alex.

Missy ducked away, knowing what was coming.

Alex's body jerked and twisted to life in a seizure. His arms and legs flailed wildly.

Shocked by this sudden display of who knew what, Tom's face whitened and his gun hand wavered slightly. Although it was Tom who had taken Alex's file, he had never actually witnessed a seizure episode before.

Sam was out of his chair at the first jerk of Alex's spastic motor functions gone awry. He tackled Tom, who was still startled.

The gun fell and Sam kicked it across the room. Within a few minutes, he had succeeded in knocking his adversary into unconsciousness.

Quickly, Sam turned to Missy, who was standing over an unconscious Alex lying on the floor in front of the couch.

"Missy, I need your help," Sam said.

She looked up.

"I want you to take the gun out of Clara's hand. I'm going to call the police and an ambulance for Alex."

Missy sighed and nodded.

Sam left the room.

She went to where Clara was standing. "Clara, I want you to let me take the gun."

She reached for it cautiously and lifted it from the other woman's fingers.

"Good, Clara. Sit down."

Although she had relinquished the weapon, Clara didn't obey. She remained standing until Sam returned.

Sam's first action was to tie Tom's hands securely behind his back, as the man was already beginning to stir. Then Sam told Missy that a helicopter would be arriving to take Alex and her to the hospital. He also informed her that he would bring Clara as well, once the police had taken control of Tom and Doug and Gloria Johnson had returned.

"I feel so bad for Alex," Missy said. "It's been almost a year since his last episode." Then as an afterthought she asked, "Sam, can you revive Clara from her trance?"

"No, but Tom can." Sam's gaze fixed on its target.

"Snow job," Tom said curtly.

"Clara, sit down," Sam said.

This time she obeyed. "Where are we? What is happening?" Clara asked.

"It is a long story," Sam told her. "It will be explained, and things will be better from now on, I promise you. As soon as the police come, we'll need to take a ride to the hospital. But don't worry, I'll be with you. You can truly trust me. I love you," Sam told her earnestly.

Clara sighed and shook her head. "Sam, I am so confused. I don't understand."

Missy came to put a hand on her friend's shoulder. "Clara, Jesus can help you. If you're willing to trust in God first, He'll be there for you and for all who believe always."

Slowly, Clara nodded. "Yes, I want to believe."

Sam breathed a quick prayer of thanksgiving as he took out his pocket Bible to lead Clara in salvation.

At the hospital, it seemed as if the hours dragged reluctantly by as Missy waited for Alex to awaken. He had been monitored and tested in order to resume the correct medication for his epileptic condition.

Missy had tried to pray unceasingly for her beloved husband, but the stress of the morning had begun to affect her, too. Her mind wandered in a semi-dozing state. She remembered another time when Alex had sat beside her hospital bed, waiting, when they had recommitted to their love for each other following a misunderstanding after a seizure episode. Now the situation was somewhat reversed. He had experienced another seizure, but she was waiting for him.

Vaguely, Missy became aware of a masculine voice calling her name. She looked up and, recognizing him, jumped to her feet to embrace their friend since college days.

"Peter! I'm so glad to see you. Alex will be all right when he wakes up. Oh, do you know what crazy things have been happening to us—all of us?"

"Yes, yes, I've been talking to Sam. I know all about it and probably somewhat more than you do."

The red-haired man released her and explained that upon analysis, placebos had been found mixed with Alex's medication for seizures. This had caused him to miss his dosage and bring on the flu symptoms Alex had experienced. Pete further explained that subliminal messages had been found on Clara's tape. The phrase was "Don't quench the fire." Sam had explained that it must have had a special meaning that had been given to Clara during a hypnotic session.

Finally, Pete concluded by saying, "I kept trying to call Alex, or you, or even Sam. Every time someone answered the phone, the person said you were out or busy and couldn't come to the phone. Apparently no messages got to you, either."

Missy shook her head. "We were anxious to hear from you. I'm so glad you're here, Pete."

A moan from Alex brought Missy to his side.

"I'll wait outside," Pete offered.

"No, don't go," Missy replied.

"Okay. Honeymoon's over?" Pete teased.

Ignoring him, Missy spoke in a matter–of–fact tone to her husband, telling him where he was.

"I don't remember anything...anything after going to bed...at the ski lodge. You say I'm in the hospital?"

"Yes, darling," Missy answered.

"How are you doing, Alex?" Pete asked in greeting.

"Hi, Pete." Alex accepted his friend's presence as normal. He hadn't realized yet that Pete had only recently arrived. "What happened?"

"You're a hero, Alex. Your seizure startled Tom and gave Sam the opportunity to get the gun away from Clara and save us."

Alex's facial expression was a mixture of incredulity, incomprehension, and confusion.

She must have sensed it, because Missy amended, "Don't

worry, darling. We'll explain it all to you later. Just rest now. Everything will be all right, and for Clara, too. Sam will see to that."

A sneak peak at the third novel,
Whirlwind of Fear

Prologue
Cassy:

An unsettling feeling began to creep in as I started to climb the four porch steps. Something seemed wrong. Why was the para–transit driver leading me to our *front* door? Then, at the door, a large, heavy hand wrapped firmly around my forearm. I tried to resist, but the grip was too tight. I was pulled forward. My heart began to race along with my steps. I couldn't concentrate on them. They were too fast to count. Even though they were hurried, the paces were all wrong. Now my stomach was cramping too.

After a slight pause, another hand slapped my right hand onto a wooden railing and I was pulled down more steps. I hadn't had time to count these either. This situation was spiraling out of control like a whirlwind running rampant. Then the reality hit like a slap...*This wasn't my house!* My heart was pounding furiously now as I was pulled across a level surface. Then the hand gripping my left arm released it.

Once the whirlwind of motion had stopped, I knew I was alone when the air was sucked away from me and the sharp cigar smell receded. Once all was still, except for the pounding of my heart, I tentatively raised my hands and stepped forward slowly, cautiously. My hands flattened against a smooth wooden surface. The door felt hard and unyielding. Groping around, I found the smooth, cold knob and grasped it. My heart began to pound faster. Logically I knew that it would be locked, but maybe...just maybe...it hadn't closed all the way? Maybe…I could...pry it...somehow? Gathering a deep breath, I slowly tried to turn the cold round thing in my sweaty hand. It would not obey my fingers. Then I twisted harder, pulled, pushed. It was, after all, locked.

With a resigned sigh I turned to explore my new surroundings. Had the para-transit driver dropped me off at the wrong address? This had to be some horrible mistake. My breath caught in my throat. What if that wasn't a *real* driver! But the van had been real. I knew its layout. What if someone had pretended to be a transit driver...but how could that happen, and why? A shiver ran down my back. My mother would be so worried.

Thoughts of my parents began to creep into my mind. I shuddered and shook my head. My breath became short and shaky. Would ma have called dad by now? The police? No, I chided myself not to think of them, for then I would surely collapse into a sobbing heap. They love me and would be so frightened. They had always protected and supported me, been patient with me, given me comfort and much love.

Think of something else, I told my mind as my throat began to tighten again. Come on, girl, you're smart, I told myself in my mind. After all, I was an honor student and a senior in high school. I'm seventeen, almost an adult. Would I get the chance to become an adult? What was this about? I asked myself as my breathing again became ragged. Why have I been taken to this place? What place?

Abruptly I began to feel along the walls. They were cold and rough, made of cement. There was also a damp, musty smell too, I realized. This must be a basement room. Slowly I walked along each of the walls, traveling to my left from the closed and locked wooden door. This would be my main point of reference. I took a deep breath and tried to concentrate.

Near the farther end of the third wall, I came to an open space. This startled me at first. I reached one hand into the air space, then around the frame of another wooden door. Beyond the frame the wall was smooth and cool. This was a tiled wall. I stepped inside the room and stretched both arms out at my sides. I could touch both walls, both smooth. I stepped forward slowly. My stomach bumped into something hard. I lowered my hands to discover a small sink with two faucets. Stepping around this I then bumped against what I had expected to find-- a toilet. I had a bathroom! Relief. Was there a shower or tub? I trailed along the wall past the toilet, turned and came to a shower stall. Was there a window?

I turned back to the shorter wall between the toilet and the shower. I reached up but felt only solid wall. I felt no air coming off of it. No window here. Surely there must be at least one window somewhere? I decided to go back along the walls again feeling for some hint of air flow. Wait, there should be one more wall. Yes, I hadn't gone full square yet. I continued past the corner to the final rough cement barrier.

This wall felt colder than the others. I stood still with my hands pressed against its craggy surface. Then I turned my face upward, standing very still. Yes, I felt a very slight hint of coldness. Was I imagining it? I reached up with one hand. There had to be a window above my reach. Could I find something to reach it? Could I open this and find my way out?

Hurriedly now, I paced along this wall, turned the corner

and continued until I came to the locked door where I had begun my trek around the outer perimeter of the room. Now, with renewed purpose, I focused my exploration on the inner area of my private prison.

Lightning Source UK Ltd.
Milton Keynes UK
UKHW010654240621
386081UK00010B/504